Love You Forever

You have to fight
your own battle!

[signature]

Love You Forever

ABBYSHEK CHANDRA

Srishti
PUBLISHERS & DISTRIBUTORS

Srishti Publishers & Distributors
Registered Office: N-16, C.R. Park
New Delhi – 110 019
Corporate Office: 212A, Peacock Lane
Shahpur Jat, New Delhi – 110 049
editorial@srishtipublishers.com

First published by
Srishti Publishers & Distributors in 2019

10 9 8 7 6 5 4 3 2

Printed and bound in India

To the love of my life,
Vagisha

Contents

Acknowledgement

I am indebted to the following people for their love and support:

Arup Bose, Publisher, for deciding to publish this novel and helping me reach millions of readers through a credible platform like Srishti.

Mr Jayanta Kumar Bose for his belief in me.

Stuti, my editor, for her valuable feedback in making the novel much better and crisper than it originally was.

Vagisha, my wife, for tolerating my obsession while I lived the life of the characters of the novel. Without her feedback, this novel would not have been possible. She deserves full credit for turning me into an author.

Prof K.C. Sinha and Mrs Indu Sinha, my parents, for their unconditional love and support in letting me chase my dreams. They have made me what I am today.

Ryan and Sean, my sons, for listening to my stories every night and showering me with their love.

1

September 2016
Dubai

"Daddy, I want Mumma," demanded my four-year-old son Rey yet again as I tried to put him to sleep.

"Sleep, Rey! When your Mumma was there, you always wanted Daddy, and now when she is not here, you want Mumma? She got very angry with us because we were bad boys, and left us," I replied in a voice that reflected a mix of anger, frustration and sorrow.

"Daddy, why are you angry? Why are you showing big eyes to me? If I don't sleep, will you also leave me?" Rey asked.

"I am not angry, son. Daddy loves you and he will never leave you like your Mumma did. Don't worry, and please go off to sleep," I said.

"Rey will sleep with Daddy… only Daddy, no Mumma. Mumma is a bad girl," Rey responded noticing my expression.

"Life will be easier for both of us if we assume she was a bad girl and an escapist. Now go off to sleep," I said.

Rey was a very caring son. He could not see me angry or sad. And if he did, he would hug me, kiss me and act funny in front of me to make me laugh. In fact, in this case, he was very much like his mother, Myra. But Myra had betrayed me. I just hope Rey does not.

Both 'love' and 'entrepreneurship' are flashy words. As a lover or an entrepreneur, you are in an enviable position from anyone else's point of view. The enviable situation changes to a pitiable one when you look at your life from your own point of view. Believe it or not, it is a fact, no matter how much any lover or entrepreneur denies it. You pay a huge price in the form of sacrifices to be successful in both. While you light up your outer world with your personal/ professional success, only you know how dark your inner world is. My story is no different. From outside, I appear like a bright light illuminating the world, but from inside, I am nothing but a fused bulb.

I did not feel like sleeping that night. I used to love sleeping and snoring my lungs out until a year ago, till my life took a turn, that made my worst fear come true. That's when things changed forever. And it was I, Abby, who was responsible for it.

I went into the balcony of my study to smoke. I might have taken a couple of drags when the unpredictable Dubai rains started falling. As I scurried back in to avoid getting wet, I heard a familiar voice, "Relax Abby. Why are you running away? The rains will not burn you. It is water, not acid." My wife, rather my ex-wife Myra, used to tell me this whenever I ran for shelter during the rains. I loved her so much, but she had ditched me. I will never forgive her for that.

I crashed into my rocking chair and started reminiscing about my past. As episodes of my life started flashing before my eyes, tears started to roll down my cheeks.

2

May 2000 – June 2001
Patna

I was in Class XII, preparing for the dreaded IIT Joint Entrance Examination (JEE) in Patna, when I fell in love with my umpteenth girl. For all the other women earlier, my love was solely based on physical attributes, but this time, it was different.

It was the year 2000 and I had joined Prof Verma's Organic Chemistry Coaching Classes. Since the classroom was small and students many, the benches and desks were arranged very close to each other to accommodate them. I was assigned a seat on the third bench with three of my school friends. To my delight, the first two benches were assigned to girls.

"Wow!" I had said on the very first day of class when I saw girls sitting closer to me than ever.

"Shit!" I had said, embarrassed, the same day when the professor asked me a simple question and I gave him a very stupid answer.

Well, that was the last time I could not correctly answer a question in class. From the second class onwards, I was always the first one to answer the Professor's questions. So, I had the impression of a very intelligent student in class.

Talking about my physical appearance, I was about five feet eight inches tall with an athletic body and wheatish complexion. I think I looked quite similar to actor Rajeev Khandelwal. Even though I was very particular about the way I looked, I felt helpless with my below average face. But that did not stop me from fantasizing about women. Bound by habit, I noticed the girls sitting in front of me. One of them really caught my attention. Unlike the other three, she was pretty and curvaceous, with beautiful brown eyes and lips to die for. You could call her the Indian version of the Hollywood actress, Alicia Silverstone. Her name was Shalini.

During the lectures, I would often observe Shalini. Though her assigned seat was diagonally in front of me, she would always sit right in front of me. Even on days when she came in late to class, she would wade her way through the jam-packed classroom to sit in front of me, on the seat that was not hers.

More often than not, her back rested on my desk. At times, when my hand would inadvertently touch her back, both my hands would at once swing into action to cover my cheeks, to minimize the impact of an impending slap from her. But neither did she slap me, nor did she complain to the professor. I tried to avoid any deliberate physical contact with her, but you can imagine how tempting it would have been for me.

For the next few months, whenever we got a chance, Shalini and I started exchanging cute glances, often followed by smiles. I used to tell myself, "*Hansi to fansi.* If she smiles, she is trapped!" As days passed, the intensity and frequency of her stares and smiles increased. I started analyzing the signals and that led me to believe that she felt for me what I felt for her – love.

My interaction with girls were limited to my dreams, wherein I had done with them everything my creative little mind could think of. In the real world, I was too hesitant to even talk to them. I was not diffident, but somehow, I could never muster the courage to talk to the opposite sex. Added to that, my shyness was like an icing of shit on my cake of love.

"See Abby, there have been instances before when a couple of girls have smiled at you. You never talked to those girls and so, you will probably never get to know their feelings for you. You can only guess. Do you also want to keep guessing Shalini's feelings? You have two options. One, take a chance this time and directly ask Shalini. Two, ignore it and live your entire life in ignorance," the inner Abby (my inner self) said to me.

"Decision taken. Let's take a chance this time," I replied.

I immediately started planning my first interaction with Shalini. Prof Verma's classes were conducted in a small room at the top floor of his residence. Shalini's father always came to drop her off and stayed there until the gates of the building opened five minutes before the class started, thus cutting down the possibility of me talking to her before the gates opened. When the gates did open, there was a rush of students, each trying to get to the classroom before the other for a reason I failed to understand, as every student had his assigned seat. So there was no scope of talking to her alone even during that time. I obviously could not talk to her during the class because the professor was always present. When the class ended, the girls were supposed to leave the classroom before the boys and Shalini's father waited for her right outside the building.

One day, before we entered the building, I turned to my three bench-mates and said, "Guys, you have to stay back here, and enter the building five minutes after I go."

"But why? What is our hero up to?" one of my friends asked.

"Well, your hero has to talk to his heroine for a couple of minutes. I will divulge the details later. For now, do as I say," I authoritatively replied, to which they acquiesced.

I hurried my way into the classroom and sat on my seat. Shalini and the other three girls were already there on their seats.

"Couldn't any of the other three girls be absent today?" I asked the inner Abby who seemed to giggle at my situation.

The benches behind me were filling up fast. I realized I had very little time before my friends and the professor entered the classroom and peed on my plan. I had to hurry. My heart was beating fast and it picked up even more pace as I tried to recall the exact line I had to say. My hands started trembling and I started shaking my legs, as if I had to pee.

I tapped Shalini's shoulder and said, "Excuse me, Shalini?"

Though my lips moved, no sound came out from my mouth. Agitated, I cleared my throat loudly and said, "Shalini, I wanted to ask you something."

"What?" she asked.

"How do I ask in front of so many people?" I said noticing her bench-mates listening to our conversation.

"Can I get your phone number?" I asked without giving her a chance to respond to my stupid question.

"No, I cannot give you my phone number," she replied rudely.

I felt a sudden gush of blood and heat to my face. Completely ruffled by her reply, I took a deep breath, opened my notebook and pretended to look through my notes as sweat droplets appeared on my forehead and my freshly sprouted moustache. It was the first time I had asked a girl for her number and she had refused bluntly. She was so loud in her reply that almost all heads turned towards me, embarrassing me to the core.

Minutes later, my friends came in and sat beside me excitedly, expecting to hear some spicy news, but as soon as they saw my face, they understood something had gone wrong and refrained from asking me anything. I was lost in my own world the entire lecture that day and kept cursing myself. By the time I returned home, I was in such a terrible mood, and so ashamed of myself that I did not want to face myself.

As always, I started talking to the inner Abby as soon as I got some 'me-time'.

"Why the hell did you make me talk to her? You should have just let it be. If she loved me, she would have come to me. What would the other students in class be thinking?" I reprimanded the inner Abby as depression started to take control of me.

"What is done, cannot be undone. At least you tried and I am proud of you for doing that. Now, don't waste time thinking about what others would think. The JEE screening examination is due in three weeks' time, focus on that," the inner Abby tried to pacify me.

For the next two weeks, I ignored Shalini completely, as if she didn't exist, and focused on my screening examination, which went well. Classes commenced after a week-long leave that we had got for the screening examination. The moment I saw Shalini's face in class, irritation filled me up. I evaded direct eye contact with her for the next few weeks as well, and then came the last day of our classes. That day, after the class, I found her waiting for me in the staircase area.

"Hi Abby! How was your exam?" she asked.

"Good!" I replied with a straight face.

"You had said you wanted to ask me something. What was it?"

"Why didn't you ask me when I tried talking to you?"

"You were talking to me in the classroom. The professor could have come in at any moment and it would not have looked good."

"I will consider that a pathetic excuse. Well, if you couldn't ask me that time, there is no point asking me right now. I don't want to talk to you," I replied rudely, but I saw her face turn sad.

However agitated I was with her, I really liked her and could not see her sad.

"Why did you always sit in front of me in class? Was there a special reason for that?" I asked her.

"No, there was no special reason for it," she replied.

"This is what I wanted to ask you. Just in case there is something you want to tell me or ask me, do it before it's too late," I said to help her propose to me.

"Sorry for being rude that day when you asked me for my number. I did not give you my number because my parents are very strict and they will kill me if any guy calls me up. You can give me your number and I will give you a call when my parents are not at home," she said.

From that day onwards, my JEE Main Examination preparations took a backseat and Shalini took the front one. We started talking over phone for close to four hours a day at different times (she gave me missed calls to signal that I could call her).

Unfortunately, Shalini and I could never meet at Patna (after becoming friends) because our parents were orthodox and we were not allowed to roam around in the city to meet whoever (especially the opposite sex) we wanted to. The law and order situation in Patna was also not good at that time. So, our love story went ahead over secret phone calls.

It was neither a crush, nor an infatuation from my side. I never fantasized about having sex with her, and only thought about spending the rest of my life with her. It was pure love and not lust. I confessed my feelings for her soon after we started talking.

"You like talking to me Shalini?" I asked her.

"Yes, I do," she replied without thinking.

"Why do you like talking to me? Who do you consider me as?"

"I like talking to you because you are entertaining and I consider you my best friend."

"Would that qualify me as your boyfriend?"

"Not everything needs to be said out aloud. There are a few things that are just understood."

"I love you Shalini, and I want to marry you," I proposed to her.

"I know, and I also want that to happen," she replied, leaving me in a state of euphoria for the next couple of months.

Before I could realize, time flew and both of us were done with taking various engineering entrance examinations. I got through JEE and enrolled for the Mechanical Engineering Course at IIT Roorkee. On the other hand, Shalini could not qualify JEE and ended up at Rajgad Institute of Technology in Karnataka.

So, I went to Roorkee and she went to Rajgad, both places very far from each other and without airports, thus eliminating the option of either of us travelling to meet the other during weekends or short vacations. During our longer vacations, both of us were supposed to travel to our hometown, Patna, where we again could not meet because of our parents and the law and order situation.

3

July 2001 – April 2004
Roorkee

It was the first year of our respective courses. Not everyone had a mobile phone in those days; it was expensive to buy and maintain one. I had one, but I soon realized I should use it only for emergency purposes, when I blew up a thousand rupees in just two days talking to Shalini. Thereafter, I usually called Shalini on her hostel's common landline number from a PCO late at night, or early in the morning because the call rates were cheaper at those times. Shalini rarely called me, but I did not mind.

Keeping up with my daily late night/early morning calls to Shalini was tough, but nothing mattered more to me than Shalini. I loved her and could do anything for her.

We also chatted on Yahoo messenger a few times and wrote emails to each other, but since her college did not have proper internet connectivity, our internet mode of communication was limited and we romanced the old-fashioned way through our love letters and landline STD calls.

I often sent her gifts with my letters, but she always lambasted me for doing so. She would get angry and bang the phone on my face for reasons unknown to me. Normally, girls liked gifts. I would then call her multiple times to apologize for sending her gifts to express my love.

The first year went by quickly, with me juggling between studies and love, and still managing to be among the 'nine-pointers' (ones who scored nine or more GPA). In the second year, however, I started devoting more time to thinking about Shalini, and this made me fumble from a nine-point 'someone' to a six-point 'no one'.

I never looked at other girls because I loved Shalini a lot and thought only she deserved my attention. I never asked her explicitly, but was confident she would never put any other guy ahead of me.

It was during our second year that she introduced me to her roommate, Shweta. From the word go, Shweta and I hit it off. I shared my feelings for Shalini with her, knowing little what that could lead to. I loved Shalini and trusted her blindly, assuming she trusted me too.

People who knew about our affair often told me, "Out of sight, out of mind Abby," a saying I played down. But as time went by, Shalini started avoiding me. Whenever I called her up, she would say she had some work or the other and disconnect.

"Shalini, what has happened to you? What is going on in your head?" I asked Shalini when I got a chance.

"Nothing, I am fine," she replied.

"No, you are not. There is some problem. Did I do anything wrong? Did I say something that hurt you? Please Shalini, tell me," I pleaded.

"Everything is fine Abby," she replied sternly.

"I am sorry. But then, why are you avoiding me?" I said in a weak voice as tears started stinging my eyes.

"I am not avoiding you. I have been a little busy with my courses and assignments, that's all. I have got to go now. Bye."

"I love you Shalini."

"Hmmm..."

"We have been in a relationship for about two years, but you have never said 'I love you' to me. Don't you love me?"

"Stop being childish, Abby!" Shalini screamed and banged the phone on my face.

She knew how much I hated people disconnecting my call when I was still not done talking, but she did it anyway. I somehow managed to blink my tears back as I came out of the PCO cabin, only to find people waiting outside staring at me. I left that PCO embarrassed and never used that PCO again during my entire stay at IIT Roorkee.

I called up Shweta and requested her to find out what was wrong with Shalini. Shweta tried her best and somehow convinced Shalini to talk to me.

"Abby, I have been avoiding you deliberately for the past few months and I am not sorry for it, because I am doing nothing wrong," Shalini called me up and said.

"I understand, you need not be sorry for anything in life Shalini. You are my goddess, and you can never be wrong. I am sorry if anything I did or said hurt you. I will change and be the one you want me to be. Tell me why exactly you have been avoiding me," I replied.

"Because I do not want to come between Shweta and you," she tried to explain.

"What? What do you mean?"

"Yes, Shweta likes you and the way you two have been bonding over all modes of communication, I think you also like her. I don't want to ruin her relationship with you and have hence decided to step aside."

"No, no, no Shalini. I have always called Shweta my past life sister. I do not like her in any other way. I have no idea where all this is coming from. Did Shweta tell you that I told her or did anything to suggest that I like her?"

"No, she did not."

"Then what made you reach this stupid conclusion? This is not a Bollywood movie in which you will sacrifice your feelings for your friend and step aside. See Shalini, this is what happens when there is a communication gap. In future, if you have any doubts related to me, talk to me directly. I love you and will never do anything to hurt you, because I don't want to lose you for anything in the world."

Though things got sorted, I had a feeling that there was more to Shalini's changed behaviour than her assumption of my affair with Shweta. The moment we ended our call that day, I decided to travel to Rajgad (that was two hours away from Bengaluru by bus) at the earliest to meet Shalini and ask her if she really wanted to marry me. The next morning itself, I went to the Roorkee railway station to book a ticket to Bengaluru (as there was no direct train to Rajgad) for the next month (May 2003) right after my fourth semester examinations. Fortunately, Shalini's examinations were to start a month after mine ended. So, I had that window of time to visit her.

I screwed up my exams yet again, dreaming about my Rajgad trip that was like a pilgrimage to me. I told my parents that one of my friends had invited me to his brother's wedding in Bengaluru and I would be going there for a few days after my exams. Though unconvinced, they allowed me to go.

When I reached Bengaluru, Shalini was there to receive me. She was dressed in a tight-fitting white ethnic suit that accentuated her curves. The idiot that I was, I did not hug her; we just shook hands. People would call me a dickhead, but I think I was innocent. We then left for Rajgad in a bus.

"How have you been Abby?" she asked as I sat beside her.

"I have not been that good, but right now, I am better than I ever was," I replied taking deep breaths, trying to control my pulse that was racing.

She kept blushing throughout the journey while I kept looking at her with admiration. Nothing else in the world existed for me. Trust me when I say, I was looking only at her face and not lower down her body. Slowly, I took her hand into mine and said, "I love you Shalini, and I cannot live without you."

It was the first time we were meeting properly and both of us were ecstatic from inside. Two hours passed like two minutes and we reached Rajgad. She had booked a room for me at a guesthouse near her hostel. I checked in and freshened up quickly while she went back to her hostel to freshen up. We met exactly an hour later at the guesthouse, after which she took me around her college campus and then to a restaurant, where nearly ten of her female friends were waiting to meet me over dinner.

After dinner, Shalini left with her friends for her hostel and I returned to my room. Early the next morning, we left for Bengaluru. It was then that I told her my reason for coming to Rajgad.

"Shalini, do you know why I am here?" I asked.

"To meet me," she replied innocently.

"Yes, but more importantly, to ask you a question," I replied.

"Then ask," she blushed.

"I love you a lot, Shalini. I will never ask you to go against your parents and marry me. But if your parents ask you to marry me, will you do so?"

"Yes, I will."

"Great! You do not need to tell your parents anything about us. My parents or I will go and talk to them, but when they ask you whether or not you want to marry me, you should not back off."

"I will not."

Hearing that reply, I breathed a sigh of relief, for my trip's mission had been accomplished. We returned to Rajgad by 8 p.m. After dinner, I dropped Shalini off at her hostel and returned to my room at the guesthouse. That day was the best day of my life until then. I still had a day with me before I left for Patna, and I wanted to make the most of it.

The next day, Shalini was occupied until late afternoon because she had a couple of important lectures to attend. After her lectures, she came directly to my room, where we had our lunch. The fact that I had to leave the next morning had already started giving me a slight headache. I started packing my stuff while Shalini sat on the couch, talking.

"Thanks for coming Abby," she said.

"The pleasure was all mine. I came here just to ask you one question, to which I have received a favourable answer," I said.

She stood up from the couch, smiled and said, "You sit down Abby. I will pack your stuff."

After the packing wrapped up, we sat on the bed and started talking. As soon as I complained of headache, she said, "Come, place your head on my lap and let me work some magic with my hands."

It was an offer I could not reject. I put my head in her lap and closed my eyes. As she caressed my forehead with her right hand, I held her left one and squeezed it a little, to which she reciprocated by doing the same. Even with my eyes closed, I could feel her face too close to mine, because I could sense and smell her breath. When I opened my eyes, she was looking at me with a faint smile on her face. I looked into her eyes that were so beautiful that I wanted to make them my home forever.

With a slight nod of my head, I signalled her to bring her face closer to mine. Her soft lips locked into mine, triggering an increased blood flow down under.

"This would be wrong, Shalini. We should not get physical before marriage. Your parents will not like it if they ever come to know of it," I said as I tried to control my physical desires and move away from Shalini, who was literally trembling.

I could clearly see the nervousness on her face because of the kiss and I had no intention of taking advantage of her moment of weakness.

Before we could realize, it was 10 p.m. and we had just one hour left for her hostel curfew. We had our dinner quickly, after which I dropped her off and returned to my room to doze off.

The next morning, I was woken up by polite knocks on my door. When I opened the door, I saw Shalini.

"Good morning Abby. You are still sleeping?" she said.

"Hey, good morning. I could not have asked for a better visitor so early in the morning. Come in, I will get ready in a bit," I replied.

In a matter of a few hours, we were at the Bengaluru railway station. My train arrived and Shalini boarded it with me to help me arrange my luggage. When both of us sat on my seat for a few minutes to catch our breaths, a lady on the opposite seat asked me, "Is she your wife?"

"Yes, she is," I replied, trying to live my dream in which Shalini was my wife.

"Abby, let's go out onto the platform otherwise the train will start moving and I will not be able to get down," Shalini blushed and said.

"I am the happiest person on earth right now. I also got to call you my wife today. It was a lovely feeling," I told Shalini excitedly as I got down from the train with her to say bye to her.

"I saw your face when you said that. You are very naughty," she said.

"That I am," I said as the platform signal turned green for my train.

"I love you Abby," she said and hugged me tight before I could decide whether or not we should hug.

"I have been dying to hear these words from you. I love you too, Shalini. Take care and never change," I replied, hugging her back.

After spending my remaining vacation in Patna, I returned to Roorkee and was doing well in my fifth semester, rejuvenated both physically and mentally due to my Rajgad visit. Shalini, on the other hand, stayed back at her college during the vacation for some project and was doing just fine in her fifth semester. We were having regular telephonic conversations like we used to.

The bad thing about good situations is that they do not last long and my case was no exception. Shalini started avoiding me again. Though I told her that I rarely talked to Shweta, or any other girl for that matter, and so, she should not worry, her behaviour still continued. My plan (with regard to Shalini and my marriage) was to talk to my parents as soon as I got a job during our campus placements at the start of my fourth year, and convince them to talk to Shalini's parents for our marriage. I knew it was too early to talk about marriage, but Rajput girls generally got married very early and I did not want to take any chance of losing Shalini to a guy chosen by her parents. If Mom-Dad showed any reluctance in talking to her parents, I would talk to her parents directly. But Shalini's current behaviour really had me worried and thinking about my plan.

My heart compelled me to call Shweta, but she said she had no clue about Shalini's weird behaviour. I recalled Shalini once calling me from a mobile number that belonged to her sister, Tanisha. Since I had her number saved, I called her, but even she had no idea why Shalini was acting strange.

I did not even have an inkling of what was going on in Shalini's head and the ignorance was eating me up from inside. I was already screwed up academically, and now, I was screwed up personally too.

My sixth semester started in January. Things changed, but for the worse. Shalini and I now talked once every three days, and that too, for not more than five minutes. The good thing about bad situations is that they too (like good ones) do not last forever. This is why I was hoping everything would fall back in place and life would again be happier than ever.

Before too long, I was staring at my sixth semester examinations that were due in the next three days. In the afternoon, when I was busy studying in my room, I received a call from Tanisha.

"Hey Tanisha, how have you been?" I asked.

"Hey Abby, I am good. How have you been?" Tanisha replied in a low volume.

"What's wrong Tanisha?" I said in a concerned voice.

"Nothing, I just called to inform you that Shalini's marriage has been fixed to a boy based in Bengaluru," Tanisha said hesitatingly.

"What? Are you kidding me? How is it possible?" I was stunned.

"Everything happened very fast, Abby. You know how such things happen in Bihar. The groom's side saw her photo through a common distant relative and liked it very much. They approached Mom-Dad for the marriage and convinced them for it. The *roka* has already been done. I don't think anything can change this decision now."

"Thanks for the call Tanisha. Catch up with you later, bye," I said and disconnected.

I was brimming with anger. Shalini should have been the one to call me and tell me what had happened, not Tanisha. I immediately called at Shalini's hostel number, but was told that she was not there. Desperate and restless, I then called Shweta on her newly-purchased cell phone, but she disconnected and messaged that she was in a lecture.

Three hours passed. There was still no call from Shalini. At around 6 p.m., I called Shweta again on her mobile. I knew that Shweta and Shalini met around this time every day, after their classes, to have snacks together at their hostel cafeteria.

"Give the phone to Shalini," I said.

"She is not here," Shweta replied.

"I know she is there with you Shweta. Now give the phone to her," I yelled.

"Yes Abby, tell me," Shalini said taking the phone from Shweta.

"What have I just heard Shalini?" I asked.

"You have heard it, so you tell me," Shalini said.

"Your marriage is fixed?"

"Yes, it is true."

"Why didn't you call me and give me this news earlier? Tanisha called me up instead, and told me everything. In fact, you were not even bothered about calling me; I called you."

"It just happened very fast and I would have called you tonight."

"Didn't tonight seem too early for it? You should have thought about calling me after your wedding," I said sarcastically.

"You should have at least informed me a day before the roka. I could have done something," I continued.

"I told you Abby, everything happened too fast. Even I was not informed and I came to know of it only today," she tried to explain.

"And you did not object to it, Shalini? You said 'yes' to it? Didn't you want to marry me?" I asked her, but got only her silence in reply.

"Listen Shalini, you still have to do nothing but give me a go-ahead to talk to your parents. Trust me, I will not marry you if they say 'no' to our marriage, but at least let me give it a try. Allow me to talk to your parents or I will ask my parents to talk to yours and everything will be fine," I kept talking.

"Everything has already been finalized and all our relatives have been informed. Nothing can be done now," she said.

"Since you are not allowing my parents or me to talk to your parents, the least I expect of you is to show some respect to our love and tell your parents about our relationship. Do not let our love down, Shalini."

"I said nothing can be done, Abby."

"I will not be able to live without you Shalini. I love you more than anything else in this world. Please, please, I beg of you, talk to your parents at least once, for me."

"Shut up, Abby. I cannot hurt them for you. Don't call me ever again because I am getting married now and it will be morally wrong of us to talk to each other," she said and disconnected the call without giving me a chance to respond.

I was appalled. How could a girl who I loved so much and who apparently loved me too, do this to me? I had been brutally dumped with a lame reason that was difficult to accept. I was left with sore feelings of betrayal and rejection, and a torturous set of unanswered questions – What is the real reason why she is dumping me? Does she not love me? Is she seeing somebody else and the roka is imaginary, just to get rid of me?

Still in shock, I sat on the bed, controlling my tears, and tried to relax myself by listening to the inner Abby.

"Abby, relax! I know it's a tough time for you, but think about it. Would you like to spend the rest of your life with someone who never cared a bit about your feelings and who is not ready to talk to her parents about you even once? She is not even letting you talk to her parents. It is obvious, she does not love you. She has always made your life miserable and has never shown any respect either for you or for your love. If you shed even a drop of tear for a girl like her, you will be doing injustice to that drop. Her rejection is her loss, not yours. You have your examinations in three days. Channelize all your anger into your studies. Study hard and nail them," the inner Abby pacified me.

From then on, neither did I call Shalini, nor did she. But curiosity personified that I was, I wanted the answers to my unanswered questions. And it was not before a decade that I got them, when she made a comeback to my life, only to disrupt it one more time.

4

May 2004 – July 2005
Germany/ Roorkee

I had a very bad temper and whenever I lost it, I made sure I channelized my anger into studies. So, I took out my anger on the semester examinations and cracked them. What I also managed to do in that little time was bag a highly unlikely two-month internship in Germany, which was a big achievement in those days.

I wanted to go as far away from Shalini as possible. Being a glib talker, I managed to convince a German Professor to invite me to his University in Dresden, Germany for a two-month, fully-paid research project. Two days after my examinations ended, I left for Germany that gave me an experience of a lifetime.

It was the first time I was travelling abroad and I had no idea how I was going to manage. Though I was an extreme introvert, I started making friends in the building where I was put up. By the end of two weeks, I had made about fifteen friends (including a few students from IIT Delhi who had also come for their internships).

The thoughts of Shalini often crossed my mind, causing a heartache, but whenever that happened, I diverted my attention to mesmerizing European beauties. Though I wanted to be friends with them, I stayed away because of my typical Bihari looks.

On one of the weekends, a couple of my IIT Delhi friends and I planned a trip to Hamburg. We left for our destination on Saturday morning in a car. By the time we reached Hamburg, severe acidity, stomachache and nausea gripped me. After an early dinner, all of us were idling at a port kind of place and enjoying the beautiful sky when I felt a high tide in my stomach. Finding no public toilet nearby, I rushed to a seven-star hotel across the road. Thankfully, the security did not stop me from entering it and running to the washroom directly to address my emergency situation. The nausea also peaked into puking at the same time, making me terribly weak. It was as if I was leaking from everywhere.

When I returned to my friends, they were already up with the plan of visiting the red light area of Hamburg. Since I had visited none in my life, I got excited. As the red light area came closer and closer, the turbulent sea inside my stomach turned calmer and calmer. The recovery was so fast, and that too without any medication, that I forgot I was not well.

The red light area had numerous streets, all of which were crowded with people. Provocatively dressed women were standing at the entrance of their ground floor apartments and grabbing the arms of people passing by, quoting rates of twenty euros for a session. I was surprised at how casually women brushed their bodies past me more than a couple of times. In India, you could easily get slapped for giving or even receiving such a 'brush'. A few women even winked at me with lecherous intentions, but I controlled the man in me.

As we continued our exploratory walk on the streets, we came across a series of strip bars. Each bar had a few agents on the streets, trying to convince people to enter their bar at an entry fee of six euros. My friends were very hesitant to enter any of these bars, probably because they thought it was not the right thing to do. My principle in life had always been that right and wrong for you should not be defined by others. You only get one life and you should enjoy it doing things that you think are right. So, when one of the agents offered us to go inside his bar, have a look and pay the entry fee only if we liked what we saw, I grabbed the opportunity with both hands. I told my friends that I would sample the bar out and would call them in if I liked it. I knew if I took decisions based on their attitude and behaviour, I would miss out on an opportunity of a lifetime.

As soon as I entered the bar, I saw half a dozen female pole dancers scattered here and there. Among these dancers was a tall, voluptuous white girl who instantly caught my attention. After a minute or two of showing some dance moves with the pole, she started stripping. With each piece of her clothing that she dropped, my eyes and my mouth opened a few millimetres wider. My eyes almost popped out and my heart skipped a dozen beats when she unexpectedly (at least for me) removed the last set of clothes on her body with a sudden jerk, making her huge assets literally jump out, as if to say 'Hi' to the onlookers. It was the first time I was seeing a full grown nude woman live in front of me. Without wasting a second, I started clicking pictures of her with my eyes for my personal spank bang.

I paid the entry fees at once and sat on a chair. I shelled out another six euros for a three-minute lap dance from the same girl. I did touch the girl to feel her curves, but did nothing beyond that, because I was scared of contracting AIDS. The lap dance was sealed with a peck on my lips. When I came out and told my friends what had happened, they did not believe me and thought I was weaving stories. I guess their reaction was more to console themselves than to actually find out the truth, and I could not care less about it. The bottom line was that I had fun and was not repentant like the 'good boy' visitors to such shady places.

After a successful internship, I returned to India and spent a few days with my family in Patna before leaving for Roorkee in August for my final year. Unsurprisingly, I had topped my class in the semester examinations and become a nine-pointer again. Since I had also done my internship in Germany, everyone started looking at me as if I was a star. Little did they know that this star would soon fizzle out.

Campus placements started in the second week of August and the software biggies were the first to arrive. Their recruitment process comprised a common preliminary written test (for all the software firms that visited that year) followed by multiple rounds of interviews. Since I did not want to get into the software industry, I took the written test without any preparation, unlike my friends who had been preparing for months. At the end of the day, results of the written test were out and the list of shortlisted candidates was put on the notice board for everyone to see.

Though I was not expecting my name on the shortlist, I still felt sad when my name was missing from it, probably because most of my friends had made it to the next round of the recruitment process, while I had not. The next day witnessed multiple rounds of interviews of my shortlisted friends for various firms, and by the time the day ended, 60% of them were celebrating their placement offers from one or the other firm. It is then that depression kicked in. The companies scheduled to arrive next on campus were L&T, Tata Motors and Bharat Petroleum, but they were to come after five days. These five days were the most terrible, shameful and lonely days of my life until then, during which I did not talk to anyone and kept myself locked up in my room. I barely ate or slept, preparing for the upcoming recruitment tests, and had just one aim in my mind – getting a job anywhere and at any cost.

My situation was a perfect example of peer pressure. I was also very close to becoming a victim of herd mentality (which was joining the software industry), instead of going for my own goals in life.

For a person who had never failed in his life, failure (in the most important matters of life – relationship and job) had become the order of the day. First a failed relationship, then a failed recruitment test, and then another failed recruitment test of L&T. Yes, I failed to clear the written test of L&T too, but only partially. My situation gave the world another perfect example, this time for a popular phrase, *aasmaan se gira, khajur mein atka*.

L&T visited IITs to recruit for the post of Management Trainee (MT), which was a part of its fast track Management

Leadership Program, in which one got promotions much faster than normal employees. Quite a few of my batchmates cleared its written test and were shortlisted to interview for the post of MT. On the other hand, since I could not clear the first written test, I was asked to appear for another purely technical written test, which I surprisingly cleared. I was therefore shortlisted to interview for the post of Graduate Engineer Trainee (GET), a technical post (with a normal career progression), considered lower than MT, for which L&T recruited at lower rung colleges.

I decided to appear for the interview to gain some experience for my future interviews. The plan was to tell the interviewers directly at the end of the interview that I would not join as a GET.

The way the interview went, I knew they would select me. So, I told them directly, "Sir, L&T is my dream company, but I do not want to join as a GET. If you offer me an MT post, I will join, otherwise I will not, and I am very clear about it. If you want, you can take any number of tests for it."

"Abby, I wish I could change the company policies. You are a great guy. I think you should join us as a GET. Let me inform you that within nine months of joining, all GETs will get a chance to appear for a rigorous set of internal tests and interviews. If you are successful in them, you will get converted into an MT at par with your MT friends, without any time lag. The situation will be as good as you getting selected as an MT right now. If you are confident of your capabilities, join us," one of the interviewers made his attempt to convince me.

According to the placement policy at IIT, a job offer made to any student pushed him out of the placements. Had I said 'Yes' to the L&T people, I would have been out of the placements at once, but with a job, of course. So, I said I would think about it and left the cabin. I wanted to keep my options open because I knew I had been shortlisted for Bharat Petroleum's group discussion (GD) that was scheduled an hour later.

But then, my life had never been so simple. The GD went well and I was expecting a shortlist for the interview. When I came to see the results of the GD in the evening, I saw my name in the shortlist, but it was struck off with a pen. The reason was, L&T had selected me.

I was left with no other option but to reluctantly bow out of the placements and accept what I had been offered. Five of my batchmates got selected as MTs and I was the only one at IIT who got selected as a GET. It was an embarrassing moment for me. How could I join the same firm at a lower level with a lower salary than my friends?

I informed my parents back home about my placement. They were very happy but I could sense their excitement dampen on hearing about my package that was one of the lowest in my batch, due to which my batchmates often mocked me. I still remember what one of my friends, Ashish had said.

"*Abey* Abby, I heard you are joining L&T as a GET. How much will you be getting?" he asked, even though he knew the answer.

"I think eleven thousand per month," I replied.

"I have never seen a bigger *chutiya* than you," he said and started laughing.

"Your package is more than double of what I would be getting. You have the right to laugh at me and ridicule me. But we will see in three years from now who's earning how much. We will then decide who is the bigger chutiya." I replied to him with a smiling face, though on the inside, I was fuming with anger. This was a self-imposed challenge for me and I was ready to do anything to win and show him his rightful place.

My self-respect had taken a bad hit and was grovelling in the dust. I was gradually spiralling down into depression and had to fight back. I had no mentor who could guide and motivate me. I did not even have Shalini to pour my heart out to, and feel lighter. The only one I could talk to was the inner Abby.

"What are your career goals? What do you want to do in life?" the inner Abby asked me.

"I want to start a company of my own. I don't know when, but I want to and I will," I replied.

"How ready are you right now to start your company?"

"I don't think I am ready for it right now because I will first need an MBA to equip me with various skills needed to set up a successful company."

"For your MBA, you will need to prepare for CAT to get into any of the IIMs or GMAT to get into ISB or any other global B-school. These are two of the best options. Since the students at IIMs are mostly freshers, with no work experience, while the students at ISB or any other global B-school have an average work experience of about four years, it would make more sense to aim for the latter option because it will ensure that you have a steep learning curve. Between ISB and other global B-schools, ISB has a one-year course as compared to the two-year courses at most of the other B-schools. You don't like studying much. I think you should aim for the one-year MBA at ISB."

"But the minimum work experience required to apply there is two years. So, I will have to work for two years at L&T or some other company."

"Yes, and you will have to make sure your career progression is steep to assure the ISB admissions team that you are among the best applicants."

"Should I independently look out for a software job off campus because joining L&T as a GET is embarrassing?"

"I don't think so. If you join L&T, you know for sure that you will get a chance to get selected as MT. If you crack that, you can show a steep career graph on your resume. Another thing is, ISB looks for people from diverse backgrounds. Almost 70% of applicants to ISB are from the IT sector. If you join L&T as a Mechanical Engineer, you can develop a unique profile with which you can convince the ISB admissions team of the diversity you would bring to the class."

"So, let's join L&T and use my embarrassment as a fuel to work hard?"

"Exactly! It will be difficult, but I know you can do it."

"I will. So, L&T it is, no matter what people say. Done!"

"All the best!" the inner Abby replied and we closed one of the most important discussions of my life.

Taking the above decision was easy, but following it was very, very difficult because I had to keep myself focused and motivated continuously for the next two years.

I felt vulnerable at times and wished Shalini was still there in my life. At times, I wanted to call her up and seek answers to my unanswered questions, but my bruised heart and ego stopped me from doing so. I missed her every single day, but

I never cried for her. She had behaved heartlessly and as the inner Abby had advised, I did not waste even a drop of my tear on her. I was very angry with her and had decided I would never forgive her. Despite knowing that I was very emotional and that she was hurting me where it would hurt the most, she did not even have the courtesy to say 'sorry'. I thought I deserved that much. For some unknown reason, she did not call me even once, after our break-up call. I had no alternative but to accept the fact that she was gone. I 'shift+deleted' all my dreams of having her perennially by my side, living in the same house, sharing the same bed, raising our kids, growing old together and finally dying together.

The break-up had changed me as a person. I had become more confident and practical. From the 'emotional fool' Abby, I had become the 'practical stud' Abby, ready to use women for satisfying his physical needs and later dump them, just like most men do. But I had my regular phases of depression, which I guess god did not like. So, he gave me a booster dose of motivation in the form of two depressing news:

News 1: One of my close relatives (Rohit) from IIT Kharagpur was going to join L&T, Mumbai as an MT. The news was a painful shot in my arm. Rohit joining the same company as me, but at a higher level was going to make my life more difficult.

News 2: One of the guys from IIT Delhi who had interned with me in Germany was also joining L&T, Mumbai as an MT. It was very embarrassing for me to tell him that I was joining as a GET, more so because he considered me a stud. This news was almost as painful a shot as the first one.

It seemed as if all the people I knew at other IITs were going to join L&T, Mumbai as MTs. The final year at IIT and the summer vacation that followed passed quickly, but not before my parents questioned me on why Rohit was supposed to join in June while I was supposed to join in July. I told them that different employees have different joining dates, and there was nothing unusual about it. They did not question me on it beyond that.

I left for Mumbai in July for the next chapter of my life, fully aware of the fact that at least for the next nine months, till I became an MT (and there was no surety about it), 'embarrassment', 'frustration' and 'depression' would have a non-stop threesome in my head.

5

July 2005 – June 2006
Mumbai

I joined L&T, Mumbai in July 2005 with over six hundred GETs, all from regional engineering colleges, except two, Raj and Nimit, who were from other IITs. Knowing that I was not the lone IITian GET was a big relief.

We were spared of the usual teething troubles of finding a home and transport (to and from office) in Mumbai, as L&T provided us with a shared accommodation in a residential society and the company's free transport service. Fortunately, Raj, Nimit and I were allotted the same two-bedroom-hall-kitchen apartment.

At work, I had to make a big impact in a very short time, both for the MT shortlist and my MBA application. So, I chose the field of composites that was the most challenging and in which people were reluctant to work. I knew I would have to work very hard as the field of composites was new to India and

L&T. As expected, for the first few weeks, I was very stressed due to work because I had very little knowledge of the field I had chosen, but gradually, things settled down.

Meanwhile, frustration, depression and embarrassment were my three companions who came to drop me off at office every morning in L&T's bus in the form of Rohit and two other MTs who were my batchmates at IIT Roorkee. I used to make every effort to avoid them because their sight left me with feelings of insult and humiliation.

I came to know that MTs were called the *damaads* (sons-in-law) of the company and you know how damaads are treated in India. Most of the employees (even at senior levels) could not dare to rub them the wrong way. The MTs could go straight to the MD of the company and he would support them.

You would not be wrong if you called me jealous, the feeling was very genuine. I often cursed myself for not being serious about my preparations for the placements at IIT. However, I never let my anger, frustration and embarrassment out. Instead, I kept these emotions alive inside me because they were the ones that kept fuelling the fire in my belly.

On the night of 31 December that year, the intensities of these negative feelings peaked, probably because the world was celebrating and I had no reason to celebrate. I was a teetotaller but that night, I wanted to get drunk. I wanted to forget the world and with it, all my tensions. So, I bought myself a bottle of vodka. Raj and Nimit had their respective plans of partying out until late and had left already.

The first half of my night was spent gulping the fiery vodka and hurling abuses in the air, while the remaining half puking and spurting out undigested food. The vodka did serve its purpose though, and I forgot my tensions for a good nine hours or so. But when I woke up in the afternoon the next day, the abated feelings started bubbling again. When I went into the hall, I saw Nimit looking out of the window with a face ready to explode into tears any moment. It was obvious that Nimit (and Raj) were also going through the same intermittent phases of depression as I was.

"Hey big man! Stop making that grumpy face and tell me what is bothering you," I asked Nimit to make him feel better.

"Nothing yaar, I am just a little sad with my life," he replied.

"Sad due to the GET-MT thing?" I asked though I knew the answer.

"I believe so. Who would know better than you?" he said.

"Relax buddy! Know that this is not a matter of life and death. The best we can do in our situation is try. Thinking about the same problem again and again only increases the stress level; the problem does not get solved. We should think about the solution to that problem instead, and work towards it. That will make our lives better. We have two options – suffer defeat at the hands of our depression and frustration, or use the same feelings to fuel our determination to win over them and get back to glory. The choice is ours."

"You are right Abby. We will make a comeback to our glorious days, but the wait is killing me. There are still three months to go before the MT selection process starts. And I have heard the process is very rigorous. What if things don't turn out in our favour?"

"Well, we deserve to wait for failing the recruitment tests at IIT. Now, stop being a pessimist. If these three months pass very slowly, it is good in a way, because we will get more time to prepare for the MT tests. If they just fly off, then also it is good because we wouldn't have to wait too long for it. Both ways, we are winning, right? We have to nail it this time. Do not give yourself any other easier option because if you do, you might subconsciously want to settle for that option and stop working hard enough."

"Wow Abby! You have turned into a motivational speaker."

"I always was. Today is the first day of the year and everyone is celebrating. Let us also do something that will make us happy."

"The only thing I want to do right now is fuck the depression out of me."

"Then let's do it."

"What do you mean?"

"I mean, let some chicks fuck the depression out of us."

"And how do we get the chicks? From the chicken?"

"Very funny. That 'Strawberry Restaurant & Bar' we see on our way to L&T's bus stop, what do you think it is?"

"It is a place where food and drinks, both are served."

"Are you really that innocent or are you pretending? That is a fucking dance bar, stupid."

"You want us to fuck bar girls? Like really? That is so disgusting."

"Disgusting? What is disgusting about it? Aren't they humans? Don't demean them."

"Ok, ok, I am sorry. But Abby, I don't feel it is right."

"Who decides what is right and what is wrong? There is no universal rule book for that. Each person decides it for himself. Anything is right if you think it is right. If you tell yourself that going to a dance bar is right, you will also start feeling that way. Besides that, I am not asking you to rape the girls. We can go talk to them. There is nothing wrong in it. If you don't want to take things beyond that, it is your wish. Nobody is going to force you."

"What if the police raids the bar and arrests us? These news channels are everywhere. I would not want my parents to see me on national television like that."

"You are such a coward! These dance bars pay hefty bribes to the police so that there are no raids, and if at all there are plans of a raid, they get a tip-off."

"Ok… What about Raj? Will he also come with us?"

"Why? You need Raj to safeguard your virginity there? If it makes your decision easier, Raj has been asking me about this for months. I just have to ask him and he will be ready to go. Decide fast because Raj and I will be going to a dance bar tonight, with you or without you."

"Frankly speaking, I want to get the dance bar experience under my belt, but I am a little sceptical."

"I am assuming that's a yes."

"Yes, it is."

At 9 p.m., the three of us were standing at the entrance of the dance bar. The moment we entered the bar, our eyes lit up on seeing about ten to fifteen beautiful women and I was like, "Oh! I didn't know women customers also came to dance bars." I was always under the impression that a typical bar girl would be poor or at least would look poor. It took me a while to believe that these beautiful women were bar girls and not customers.

As one of the waiters guided us to a table, some of the girls looked at us and whispered something to each other. After settling down in my seat, I scanned the bar again. I noticed that there was a variety of women – young, old, skinny, voluptuous, fair, dusky, etc. If you wanted an eighteen-year-old fair and skinny girl, you would get one, and if you wanted a forty-year-old dusky and voluptuous aunty, you would get one too. In a nutshell, there was something for everyone there.

To be honest, I was a little nervous and scared (as were Nimit and Raj) right from the time we entered the bar. Who wouldn't be? Since childhood, I had always been advised to stay away from illegal activities, and here I was, sitting in a dance bar that ran an illegal business of prostitution. But unlike Nimit and Raj, I managed to hide it. The world sees of you only what you show. I showed confidence and the waiters called me 'Sir'; Nimit and Raj showed nervousness, and they were ignored.

I was still trying to figure out if we had to use the 'push' or the 'pull' strategy of marketing; did we have to call any girl to us (push strategy) or would a girl come to us on her own (pull strategy)? Meanwhile, Nimit and Raj were waiting for me to take the first step. I looked around at the girls and one of them caught my attention. She was a fair, full-figured, hot girl who bore a striking resemblance to the Bollywood actress Neha Dhupia. She must have been about thirty years old and looked very attractive in a slightly revealing black dress. As soon as she saw me staring at her, she made an unusually long eye contact with me. With a quick dip of my head, I signalled her to come. She smiled and started walking towards me. I was already getting aroused. To my left on the sofa were both, Nimit and Raj. She came and sat on my right.

"Hi, my name is Divya," she said in a thin, creaking tone that punctured my aroused state instantly. Her tone did not match her looks and was a big turn off. I had never thought voice could be a deal breaker.

"What have you got for me?" she said as she held my right hand and placed it on her boobs to set my pulse racing again.

The nerve cells that transmitted signals from my right hand to the brain created a short circuit in my head and repaired the 'puncture' to bring back my aroused state.

"I have got myself for you," I said in typical Bollywood style, as if I was the world's most handsome guy who she had been waiting for all these years.

"I will unwrap you later. Before that, I need a gift," she said in a slightly rude tone.

"Gift? I thought you girls dealt in cash," I said.

"If a customer wants to take me out, he has to pay me cash for my services and also gift me something, because I need to be pampered to pamper him back. You see this phone? This is worth forty thousand rupees and was gifted to me by one of the customers. You see this diamond ring? This is also a gift, that too worth thirty-seven thousand rupees. I go to such customers whenever they call me to their place. So, I need a gift and five thousand rupees cash for the night. However, there are a few not-so-beautiful girls here too; they charge much less without any expectation of a gift," she said as I quietly slid my eighteen hundred-rupees worth of phone back into my pocket.

"To be frank, I have no gift for you, Divya. I have five thousand rupees cash, if it works for you. Let me also tell you that I might not come here again. So, if you cannot spend the night with me, I can understand and am absolutely fine with it. I will be on my way back in fifteen-twenty minutes."

"You seem to be a nice guy. Why did you come here? It is not a good place for you."

"I was a little frustrated with life and wanted to try something adventurous tonight. My friends felt the same and they came along."

She looked at the two others and nodded. "Can you please find them a girl each? The girls can spend some time with them here and if they mutually decide, they can take things further," I continued.

"Sure, give me a minute," she replied.

She went and talked to a waiter and then to a few girls. Two of them agreed to give company to Nimit and Raj. She returned and asked me to shift to another table.

"Happy now?" she asked.

"Yes, I am. Thank you," I replied.

"You are not selfish. I like that."

"Thanks. You want something to drink?"

"Yes, I will order a Coke for myself."

"Tell me about yourself. I want to know you."

"I am from Durgapur, West Bengal and have been living in Mumbai with my family for the past fifteen years. Two years after we shifted here, my father passed away. I stay here with my mother and younger brother."

"Oh! I am sorry to hear that. Why didn't you people return to Durgapur after your father's death?"

"What would we do there? The opportunities looked better here than in Durgapur. So, we stayed back. As it is, my father had sold off whatever little we had there to come to Mumbai."

"Your mother works somewhere or you're the sole earning member of your family?"

"My mother used to sew clothes, but she could not make enough money to make both ends meet. Twelve years ago, when I was eighteen, a lady in our neighbourhood introduced me to dance bars. The work was dirty, but the money was good and quick. I was not literate enough to land myself a decent job. I was apparently left with no option but to get into this. After all, we had to survive somehow and we also had to send my brother to school. It is his dream to become a doctor and I will make sure he does not have to sacrifice his dreams like I had to. I always wanted to pursue my education, and then settle down with a loveable husband, have kids with him and take care of my family, but god's plan and my dreams did not intersect."

"Your mother knows you work here?"

"Yes, but she does not stop me because life has been comfortable ever since I started working here."

Our conversation was interrupted by a sudden sound of commotion coming from Raj's table. A few waiters had gathered around his table and the girl he was with was no longer sitting with him. I did not want things to turn ugly, so I asked Divya to find out what had happened, and calm things down.

"Your friend was forcing himself onto the girl. So, the girl got angry and abused him. No girl is ready to sit with him now. I think you should ask him to leave," she returned to me and said.

"I am so sorry. I will talk to him," I apologized and went to Raj.

"Raj, the bar staff is annoyed with your behaviour. I am no He-Man. I might not be able to help if these guys start assaulting you. Leave right now and save your ass. I will see you later," I told Raj, after which he left but not before being forced to cough up hefty tips to waiters who were after him like bloodthirsty hounds.

Meanwhile, Nimit was busy chatting with his girl on a separate table. So, I came back and sat with Divya again.

"Matter sorted, apologies again. I did not know he could behave like that," I told Divya.

"That's ok," she said.

"Your story makes me feel sorry for you. I wish I had more money to give you."

"It is fine. I understand."

"I have had one question in mind regarding bar girls, for quite long."

"What?"

"Do you have the option of ditching this life? Or do these bar owners and waiters keep a tab on you and you cannot just leave this job anytime you want to?"

"It is nothing like that. I can leave this job anytime I want to. There is no compulsion."

"Really? Blame Bollywood movies for creating such an impression."

I could see that Divya was enjoying talking to me. And I was also enjoying the moment because it made me forget my tensions. She held my hand and placed it on her 'thunder thighs' this time.

"You want to spend the night with me?" she asked.

"Yes, I would love to. But I don't have your gift."

"Nobody has ever bothered to ask me about my life. Customers always talk about their problems, not mine; some just have sex and leave. You are perhaps the first one who asked me about my life without sharing his problems with me. You seem to be a very good person at heart. All this while we have been chatting, you have not even attempted to touch me inappropriately. I can easily waive off your gift. You can just pay the cash."

"Thanks for whatever you said. But do not make me emotional because I might start coming here regularly to spend time with you."

"I really wish," she said with a disarming smile.

"What is the way forward?" I asked inquisitively.

"You want to go to your place or should I arrange for a room?"

"I will be more comfortable at my place and I will make sure you are too."

"You stay alone?"

"I stay with my two friends who came here with me. But you do not have to worry. We will have a room to ourselves."

"Great! Now listen, you will have to leave from the front door, while I will leave from the rear exit in an auto-rickshaw after informing the bar manager. I will ask the auto-rickshaw driver to stop outside the front door for you to hop in."

"Sure, see you."

I paid my bill and asked Nimit about his plans. He said he would stay back at the bar and call me later.

Things went exactly as Divya had said. In no time, both of us were on our way to my apartment. My abode was a typical bachelor accommodation with stuff thrown here and there. To evade the embarrassment, I scurried her into my bedroom and bolted the door from inside. Raj was probably not there at home and I least cared about where he was. I was a little pissed off with him for behaving the way he had at the bar.

"I can understand why you are in such a hurry," Divya said with a mischievous smile.

"No, no, it is not what you are thinking," I replied clarifying that I was not as restless to get laid as she was thinking.

"Liar! Let me not keep you waiting for too long. Lie down on the bed, relax and enjoy," she said, her final words turning into a whisper.

She made me lie on the bed and started undressing herself. The sight of her bare, beautiful and curvaceous body with ample fat at the right places sent ripples of excitement through my body. The fair tone of her skin was interrupted by severe bite marks. It made me pity her; she did not need to do this for a living. Anyone would have married her and she wouldn't have to make her beautiful body go through such an ordeal every night. But the point was, nobody wants to marry a bar girl, though everybody wants to fuck one. I was one of those people who would still marry her if I fell in love with her regardless of her past. But then, I had no interest in love anymore. The only girl I had loved was Shalini. Whether or not I still loved her was an extremely unpleasant question that I avoided answering, even to myself.

Divya then moved on to disrobe me and we had an experienced (at least from her side), enlightening and wild foreplay session. But while all this was happening, I had started having mixed feelings. I had planned this whole dance bar thing with the intention of it culminating in sex, but my conscience was now playing spoilsport. To me, sex was a beautiful and pure thing that denoted the union of two souls who loved each other truly and deeply. In the process of fucking my frustration out, I did not want to turn sex into something dirty. I had a feeling that I would feel terribly guilty after having sex with Divya.

The moment Divya slipped a condom onto its rightful place, I said, "Divya, I don't think I should do this. My conscience is not allowing me to go ahead. If you don't mind, can we just lie down and talk?"

"What? I knew you were different. Who takes a U-turn moments away from the ultimate gratification, to be left high and dry?" Divya said, taken aback with my sudden change of mind.

"I can only have sex with the woman I love and I don't love you Divya. I am so sorry; I hope you understand," I apologized realizing I had also deprived her of the same moment of satisfaction I had deprived myself of.

"That's ok. You are a gem of a person, do not ever change. Your wife will be very lucky."

"Thanks Divya. And don't worry, you can take the cash we agreed upon. I have no problem with that."

"I will have to, can't waive off everything, you see. This is my bread and butter. Plus, I have to give one thousand rupees commission to the bar owner."

"Not an issue. Remember to take it from me before you leave."

She lay down beside me on the bed and we started talking. Laughter filled our conversation when we read the messages she was continuously receiving from her colleague who was with Nimit in a cheap hotel room. Apparently, Nimit was not getting an erection. The girl had given up and was now giving Divya updates about the situation at her end while Nimit was working hard on himself.

Totally enervated, I slipped into deep sleep while listening to Divya. When I woke up in the morning, she was gone. Under my watch on the bedside table, was a note that read:

"I had an amazing time with you. Normally with customers, I have to feign enjoyment, but when you did things to me last night, I actually enjoyed. If I ever get married, I would want my husband to be like you, not because of your foreplay skills, but because of your nature. I wanted to say bye to you before leaving, but you were sleeping like a baby and I didn't want to disturb. I have taken one thousand rupees from your wallet to pay to the bar owner. You earned the remaining four thousand back from me. Hope to see you soon. Take care."

For some reason, I felt very good from inside for having exercised that last minute control over my desires the previous night. There was no regret. She was nice, but I had no intention of going back to her, because that would mean taking things further, which I didn't want to. The chapter on Divya was over for me. I felt like a brand new person, charged up in full to steer my life back in control.

On the other hand, Nimit's depression worsened. This happened because of three reasons. One, he could not perform the previous night. Two, he knew that I knew through Divya that he could not perform (I told him I knew the truth when he was trying to weave stories about his macho performance in bed). And three, his girl had siphoned off fifteen thousand rupees from his wallet and had vanished early in the morning while he was still sleeping.

Soon, the big day arrived and the rigorous MT selection process started. There were four elimination rounds of written tests of different patterns, as opposed to just one written test conducted at IIT. Raj and Nimit got eliminated within the first three rounds. Luckily, I qualified all the four rounds as well as the two initial rounds of interviews that followed. All of this took about two months, probably because over six hundred GETs from across the country were being evaluated and screened. My third and final round of interview also went well, but I was apprehensive about something or the other going wrong and screwing my already fucked up life further, to bury me deeper in my abysmal pit of failures.

The final results reached my boss RTR's desk a week after my final interview. RTR called one of the three GETs (in our department) who had appeared for the final round of MT selection interviews. From what everyone could see happening inside his cabin, he congratulated the GET for his selection and continued talking to him for about twenty minutes. By this time, I had started having an intuition that I had not got selected despite being from IIT and rated the best performer in my department. Had I made it, RTR would have called me first.

After the first GET came out excited from RTR's cabin, he called another GET to congratulate him. My intuition now turned into the most probable scenario – I had failed again.

I left for home right away because I could not face the embarrassment of the same failure once more. Though my colleagues tried to stop me, I left, despite knowing that it might irk RTR. Somewhere in my heart, I was still expecting a congratulatory call on my way back. But even that iota of hope got decimated when I did not receive any call for the next fifteen minutes. Instead of getting demotivated and depressed, I started planning for the next steps – a job change and GMAT.

Finally, one of my colleagues called me and said, "Abby, you need to come back. RTR needs to talk to you."

"Come back for what, consolatory messages from everyone? I am not in a position to talk to anyone right now. I will meet him tomorrow," I replied.

"Abby, you have to come back buddy. You have got selected as an MT. RTR was calling in reverse order. You were the best among everyone. Come back now."

"What? I…I…I am coming, I am coming."

GET to MT was my first step in the bigger scheme of things and I had just aced it. I had been waiting for this day for what seemed like an eternity to me. And when the day arrived, I did not know how to react. I was so exhilarated that my walk back from L&T's entry gate to RTR's cabin was fast, but clumsy.

No one can imagine the value this achievement held for me. When you achieve something you have really worked hard for, it is a feeling you have to experience to truly appreciate. I was now at par with my IITian batchmates who had got selected as MTs during the placements. I had reclaimed all that I had lost almost two years ago. I had snatched my glorious days back to be called a stud again. I could now hold my head high while traveling to office every day. I had been through a very rough patch post my break-up with Shalini, but things were starting to look up.

Everything changed. I was shifted to a one bedroom-hall-kitchen apartment (that I was supposed to have all to myself) and my salary was also hiked instantly. I was now a damaad of L&T and nobody could dare to rub my feathers the wrong way. I had always had the habit of rewarding myself for my achievements, and for my latest one, I rewarded myself with a red, hot Hero Honda Karizma bike. I could not share this good news with my parents and other relatives back home because they had no idea about the GET-MT thing and what I had gone through for about two years all alone. But I had no reason to complain.

6

June 2006 – December 2006
Mumbai

Becoming an MT was only one step towards my ultimate aim, and I could not afford to relax. I took GMAT within the next two weeks and cracked it with a score of 780/800 without any coaching.

As I had decided earlier, I applied only to ISB. Though ISB never shortlisted candidates with less than two years of work experience, I got shortlisted for the interview, probably because of my strong resume.

I had my ISB interview in the last week of October. The interview of each candidate was supposed to last for about twenty minutes, but mine lasted for an hour. And during that one hour, I was grilled on each and every point mentioned in my resume and application essays. However, I successfully managed to confidently shell out answers to all the questions. On my way back home after the interview, I had a feeling I could just might make it to ISB.

The final results of ISB admissions were to be out on 14 December, so I had more than a month's time to take things easy. The workload at L&T was also manageable. Since I was relatively relaxed, I started spending most of my time on social networking sites, especially Orkut.com.

One day, when I was browsing through Notre Dame Academy's (the best girls' school in Patna) community group, I stumbled upon the profile of a girl named "Icy".

Intrigued by her uniquely edited display picture and her profile name, I checked out her Orkut profile. She was obviously from my hometown, Patna, but was currently living in Mumbai. She was also a member of the Kayastha (my caste) community group on Orkut. Her profile showed she was one hundred and twenty-three years old. All of this increased my curiosity. I wanted to know more about her. Unfortunately, her profile's privacy settings were such that I could not see anything else, neither photos nor scrapbook (something like today's Facebook wall). Of course, I could have sent her a friend request and waited for her approval, but that could have projected me as just another creep trying to be friends with a girl. So, I controlled my emotions and thought of another strategy.

Orkut used to show last five profile visitors of one's profile every day. I visited her profile innumerable times daily for a week so that my name showed up in her profile among the last five profile visitors repeatedly. The idea behind this was to make her aware of my existence and tempt her to visit my profile. The strategy worked and her name started appearing in my profile visitors' list.

One of my biggest fears had always been being turned down by a girl, which is why I still kept myself from sending her a friend request, thinking, "What if she rejected the request? My self-respect would suffer a big blow." Thanks to her, she did something that made my life easier. I got an email update from Orkut saying, "Icy has sent you a friend request." But on my Orkut profile, there was no such request. This meant that she had sent me a friend request and then deleted it. So, I only got an email notification of the request. I was now sure she wanted to be friends with me, but did not want to make the first move. I sent her a friend request instantly, which was readily accepted.

For the next one week, we exchanged a couple of 'Hi's' and 'Hello's' on the scrapbook while simultaneously carrying out an extensive research on each other's profile. My profile had all the relevant information about me. So, she knew I was an IITian and was working at L&T, and that we shared the same hometown and caste. She could also see my pictures and knew how I looked. But contrary to my expectations, neither did her profile have any extra information about her, nor did it have any picture of her other than the edited and fuzzy display one.

When I was investing my free time in Icy, I was clear about my objective with respect to her. My intention was to chat with her, befriend her, talk to her, hang out with her till I was in Mumbai and then ditch her. And this objective was set because after being dumped by Shalini, I did not want to make any emotional investment in any relationship. I was still not over what Shalini had done to me and I was probably trying to avenge myself on every girl I possibly could.

The next step to trap Icy was to make her fall for me. I was not one of those guys who would chat with a girl on a public forum. I needed a more discrete platform to chat on so that I could work my charm on the girl in private. The solution was to migrate to Yahoo messenger. Though reluctant at first, she eventually added me on it.

"Hey, thanks for adding me," I messaged her.

"You are welcome," she replied.

"I know you were a little disinclined towards adding me here on messenger. It is not considered safe by many people."

"It is safe unless I send you my pics or videos, or share any personal information like my phone number, address, etc. By the way, this is the first time I have added a stranger on messenger."

"I feel blessed. Thanks for the favour, ma'am. But you should not trust strangers."

"Somehow, I trust you and that is why I added you. I have researched your profile on Orkut and in quite a few pictures, I saw books in the background. I read so many of your posts, the ones you wrote and the ones people wrote to you. There was no foul language anywhere, no flirting around with any girl and there was nothing obscene. You seem to be a decent guy."

"So you already know the basic stuff about me. But I don't, because your Orkut profile does not reveal much. Can you please tell me about yourself?"

"What do you want to know? I can answer questions that are not too personal."

"First and foremost, what is your name? Icy does not seem to be your name."

"It is not. My real name is Myra."

"Who do you stay with? Where do you work? What does your dad do?"

"I stay with my mom and dad. I work for a pharmaceutical company, ACG while dad is a banker. We are a normal middle class family."

"Ok... and which area do you stay in?"

"Why do you want to know that?"

"So that anytime I am around that area, my eyes can look for you."

"I live in Lokhandwala, Andheri West."

"Thanks, not for telling me your area, but for trusting me."

"There is something in you that makes you stand out from the rest."

"And what is that 'something'?"

"I don't know, just something."

"Thanks! You are cute."

"I know I am. The doorbell rang, I think it is my dad. I will chat with you later."

"What? Why? Are you scared of your dad?"

"Yes, I am. If he gets mad, you can't even imagine what he can do."

"But you are not doing anything wrong. Why will he go mad? We are not having a sex chat."

"Censored," she replied and signed out. It was the word 'sex' that triggered that reply from her. And this remained the case whenever she got a sniff of sex or anything physical in our conversation. 'Censored' is what she would say and immediately change the topic. On the one hand, it irritated me, but on the other, it threw light on her good character and cultured upbringing.

We started chatting regularly on messenger but only when both of us were at our respective homes, because messenger was blocked in our offices for obvious reasons. Our chats were platonic. We chatted to each other about our family members, our daily routine and about other general stuff with no dirty talks, thanks to her 'censored' nature. The next step for me was to get her phone number. Knowing her, I was sure she would not share her number so easily. So, I worked out another strategy.

"Hey Myra, how was your day today?" I messaged her on messenger one day.

"It was good. I had a lot of work related to the exhibition ACG is participating in. How was your day?" she replied.

"It was hectic. I actually should have stayed back at office until late today to finish preparing my presentation that I have to make tomorrow. But I came back home so that I could chat with you. You have become a good friend and I look forward to chatting with you every day," I wrote and I really meant it.

"The pleasure is all mine. Now, you finish preparing your presentation first, then we will chat."

"I can't do that at home. I need to insert a few snapshots from a design software in the slides and that software is installed on my office computer, not on my personal laptop."

"Oh! We could have chatted later Abby. Work is important and it cannot wait; I can. You should have stayed back at office and finished your work."

"Maybe it is not that important for you to chat with me every day, but for me, it is."

"I did not mean that. I, too, look forward to chatting with you. But I don't want your work to suffer because of me. How will you finish your work now?"

"I will go to office early morning tomorrow and wrap things up. Don't worry, I will handle it."

"Are you sure?"

"Absolutely! But there is one issue."

"What?"

"I have a weakness. I cannot get up early in the morning by myself. When the alarm rings, I switch it off and go back to sleep again, thinking that I will get up in five minutes, but those five minutes turn into an hour or even more."

"Ask your flatmate to wake you up."

"He is worse than me. He is deaf to all alarms."

"Oh!"

"9004340005 is my phone number. I am not asking you for your number as I understand your security concerns. Just in case you can, call me from any phone in the world at 6 a.m. Stop calling me only when I pick up the phone and tell you that I am wide awake. In any case, I am not forcing you to wake me up. Do not get tensed about it. It is absolutely fine if you can't."

"I don't wake up so early in the morning. So, I will not promise anything."

"Yeah, I understand. No problem. I will try to wake up on my own. I just hope I do."

My last message was meant to make her think that I was not expecting a call from her the next morning. But I knew she was very caring and she would call me, that too from her personal mobile phone and I would get her number. As expected, she called me the next morning and I got her number.

That very day, we shifted the platform of our conversations from computers to mobile phones. We started talking over the phone throughout the day and the 'knowing each other' phase gave way to the 'desire to see' phase. So one day, I asked her for her picture.

"Hey Abby, good morning," she said as soon as she received my call.

"Hey Myra, morning. Busy?" I asked.

"Not for you. Tell me. Anything urgent?"

"Nothing urgent. I just wanted to hear your voice."

"No work right now?"

"Not really."

"Something is going on in your head. Tell me."

Myra had this knack of knowing whenever something would be going on in my head. And she would not let go of me until I told her what it was.

"What? I am not thinking about anything. Trust me, I am blank in my head right now," I made a futile attempt to convince her.

"Abby, we have interacted so much in the last one month that I know you quite well now. If you do not tell me what you are thinking about, I will not talk to you."

"What the hell Myra! Ok, I was just thinking that you know how I look, but I still have no clue what you look like."

"You will see me at the right time, don't worry."

"I am not worrying. It is just that when I think about you, I cannot imagine your face, your body, etc. So, I am not able to picturize any situation with you. It is not that I am asking you for your photo or something. I don't know, let it be. I will be fine in sometime. You tell me, how is the workload today?"

"Abby, you are not a stranger anymore. I will click and email you my pic in some time. Now, stop thinking about it."

"I just can't wait for your email. I am signing into my email account right away. Bye."

"Hey, relax! I will take ten minutes to do that. I will click a picture with my phone, transfer it to my computer and then email it to you."

"I am waiting for it already."

After a long wait of ten minutes, her picture reached my inbox. It was not a full-length picture, so I could not check out her body proportions, but I could see her face and that she was dressed in a pink saree. She was fair and looked a lot like Selena Gomez. The adjective 'hot' automatically suited her. I would be lying if I said I didn't compare her with Shalini. Both Myra and Shalini were different in their looks, each beautiful in her own way. Myra was a great combination of western beauty and hot looks, while Shalini was more of an Indian beauty.

"Thank you so much. You look so pretty," I called Myra immediately and told her.

"Thank you Abby. It is traditional day at office today. The picture is not clear because I clicked it with my phone, but it is still decent enough to give you an idea of how I look. Now cheer up!" she said.

"I am grinning from ear to ear. Thanks Myra!"

"Have to go for a meeting now. Will catch up with you later. Take care, bye."

"You too. Bye."

An important date in my life was about to arrive – 14 December, the day when my ISB admission results were to be announced. Anxiety and tension overshadowed my thoughts about anyone else, including Myra. It was in my nature that whenever I was nervous or stressed, I preferred staying alone and talking to myself to lift my spirits. So, I stopped talking to Myra for a few days. She had no idea about my MBA plans and ISB application. She had never asked me and I had never told her.

On 14 December, somewhere in my heart, I was expecting a congratulatory call from ISB. But to my disappointment, I didn't get any.

Though the chances of my failure were high because of my work experience and I knew it, I was still feeling embarrassed that I could not make it and wanted to disappear from this world. I skipped my dinner and locked myself up in my room to get some pep talk from the inner Abby.

"You already knew you would get rejected," the inner Abby remarked.

"I agree I knew it. But if number of years of work experience had come in the way of my selection, ISB would not have shortlisted me for the interview in the first place. I am clueless as to what went wrong because I think my interview went really well, and that is what had made me a little hopeful," I said.

"Let it be. What has happened has happened. You apply to US B-schools next year. Everything happens for the best. Relax and enjoy the next one year. For now, stop thinking about the reason of your failure."

"Yeah, everything happens for the best."

The feeling of having failed was still pulling me down. I started researching on the US B-school applications and dozed off with my laptop still on, at around 4 a.m. I woke up three hours later and found my laptop staring at me with an email from ISB.

It was an email congratulating me for my selection. I could not believe what I read, and at first, I thought the email was sent by mistake. So, I checked the name the email was addressed to. I then logged onto my ISB applicant profile on ISB's website to confirm that the email was not an error made by ISB. I had to recheck my email and my applicant profile thrice to believe that I had indeed made it to ISB. Without further ado, I called Mom and Dad, who were as proud of me as I was of myself.

I then called Myra.

"Hi Myra! Good morning," I said.

"Hi Abby! Good morning. How come you called so early in the morning? I am still to get out of my bed," she said in a sleepy voice.

"I have to give you some good news."

"What are you waiting for?"

"I had applied to ISB for my MBA and I made it."

"ISB? Which college is that?"

"You have not heard about ISB? Are you serious?"

"I have heard about IIMs but have no idea about ISB. Since you are so excited about it, it must be a good college."

"Good college? It is one of the best ma'am. In fact, there is an India-Pakistan kind of rivalry between ISB and IIM Ahmedabad. It is that good, or even better."

"Oh, is it? Congratulations!!! So sorry, I should have wished you before asking irrelevant questions. This calls for a treat."

"For that, you will have to meet me. When are you meeting me?"

"I don't know."

"What do you mean? You don't want to meet me? My birthday is next month, on 24 January. You want to meet then? I can come to your office or wherever you say."

"I mean I am not sure. I will have to think about it."

"Why are you acting so pricey? If you don't want to meet, it is fine. It is not that I am dying to meet you. In fact, just let it be. I don't want to meet you now. You stay safe and secure, and distrust every guy. Bye."

"Abby, listen to me...." I disconnected the call without letting her finish.

Though I talked to her regularly and was now asking her to meet me, I was still very clear in my head about Myra. I did not want to take our relationship further as I was not ready for it. I admit I used to imagine her in different situations with me, but those situations were just meeting her at some coffee shop or a pub. So in a way, she was right in being unsure about meeting me because she had no future with me. Despite being unambiguous about my 'no future with Myra', her response to my proposal to meet still pissed me off big time, because it hurt my ego.

While I was busy celebrating my success, Myra was busy calling me and apologizing to me through text messages and emails. Though I told her I was not angry when she apologized multiple times, I decided to limit my interaction with her before vanishing from her life once I left Mumbai for ISB Hyderabad in a couple of months. I was not emotionally attached to her, so it was not going to be a big deal for me.

I was happy, very happy about getting through ISB and was basking in the glory of my success. I had never been a fan of studying. ISB was going to be my last degree, after which, no one would ever ask me to study again.

7

December 2006 – January 2007
Mumbai

My interaction with Myra over the next two weeks was very limited. Our phone calls that used to last at least half an hour, now lasted for only a few minutes. But then came new year's eve, jumping into our lives.

Raj was going to a popular mall named Infinity in Lokhandwala. He asked me to come along and I agreed, as I was free. Realizing I was in the same locality as Myra's, waves of excitement started propagating through my body.

It was a Sunday and there was every chance of her being in the same mall. With an untrimmed and overgrown beard, I was in my bathroom slippers. Obviously, I was not looking my best. So, I did not want to meet her, but I wanted to know if she was around. If she was, I would look out for her and analyze her looks from a distance without letting her know of my presence.

"Hi Myra, how are you?" I called Myra.

"I am fine. What about you?" she replied.

"I am good. Where are you?" I asked her to check where she was.

"I am downstairs in my building, talking to my friends. Why? Where are you?" she asked.

"How far is this mall named Infinity from your place?"

"Why? Are you at Infinity mall?"

"No, I was just asking."

"Don't lie! You are there, right? Swear on me and say you are not at Infinity mall."

"Ok, I am at Infinity mall, but I am leaving from here now." I told her the truth. I did not believe in the 'swear on someone' thing, but I never took a chance with anyone's life because of my beliefs. What if falsely swearing on someone actually killed her? So, I told her the truth.

"I am coming. Give me five minutes."

"No, no, no, Myra. I am leaving. We will meet later."

"You be there for five more minutes, please."

"Listen Myra, the point is that I am not dressed appropriately and am looking like a beggar. We will meet later. Trust me, I am not angry with you. Next time, when I am in this part of the city, I will surely meet you."

"Looks do not matter to me. Wait there for five minutes, I am already on my way," she said and disconnected the call before I could say anything.

I rushed to the restroom to wash my face and set my hair to look a little decent.

"Where are you? I am on the second floor of the mall, right in front of the bookstore named Landmark." She called me after five minutes.

"Give me two minutes. I am coming," I replied.

When I reached Landmark store's entry, I noticed a cute girl standing and impatiently scanning every face she could see in the mall, one by one. Since I came from the side, she did not see me coming.

"Hi Myra!" I said.

"Hi," Myra said and started giggling.

During our extended handshake, she kept smiling and looking into my eyes while I was busy scanning her. She was dressed in a short denim skirt and a pink floral spaghetti top. Just like in her picture, she was a replica of Selena Gomez. She was very fair and with shoulder-length hair and a smile to die for, was much more beautiful in person than she was in her picture. Not to forget, she had very beautiful legs. We met for not more than three to four minutes and did not talk beyond our exchange of 'Hi's'. We went down the escalator together and parted ways with a 'bye'. Within minutes of going our separate ways, she called back.

"You look so different than you do in your pictures," she said, stealing my words.

"You too. You look more beautiful in person," I replied.

"Thanks. Going by your pictures, I had thought you would be six feet tall, very broad and muscular, but in person, you look like a school-going kid."

"Even I had expected you to be tall and voluptuous, but you are so small. When we shook hands, I felt like a giant in front of you," I said, thinking she was being critical of me despite me complimenting her on her looks.

"Abby, I did not mean it in a negative way. You look cute."

"Ok, I take my words back. You talk a lot on the phone, but in person, you don't speak at all."

"Arre, I did not know what to say. But what about you, mister? You didn't have a mouth to talk or what?"

"I was busy observing you. Our time was limited too. We need to meet again. It is 1 January tomorrow. What are your plans? Office?"

"There is a holiday tomorrow. As of now, I have no plans. I will be staying at home only."

"Do you want to meet up somewhere? Let's say Inorbit mall at 11 a.m.?"

"Ummm...done! I will be there."

The next morning, we met at Inorbit mall. She was wearing a nicely fitted, blue low-waist jeans, and a black top short enough to reveal her beautiful flat tummy. I was better groomed as compared to the previous day, with trimmed beard and slicked back hair. I was wearing blue jeans and a blue slim fit t-shirt, both of local brands.

We chose to sit in the food court for some time, where she gave me the gifts she had bought for me – a novel, a pen and a Davidoff Cool Water perfume. It was very thoughtful of her to bring these specific gifts. I loved buying books (not reading them though), I loved pens (a pen as a gift always worked for me) and I loved perfumes. During our conversations on phone, I had mentioned these things, but I had least expected her to remember and get them for me. On the other hand, I had come without any gift, dangling my empty hands on my sides. I had my reason for this shameless behaviour. I did not want to take things further with her and hence, did not see any sense in investing in her.

We started talking about the mall, the stores it had, and simultaneously gorged on the dosas we had ordered. Our conversation was frequently interrupted by phone calls coming on her cell phone during which I observed her. She had silky, dark brown tresses flowing down to her shoulders, perfect for a shampoo advertisement. Beautiful pink lips adorned her face with long, curvy eyelashes that preceded an engaging set of very communicative and mischievous eyes. Her hands were well-moisturized and manicured. I subjected a few more of her body parts to my scrutiny, and found them almost perfect in every aspect. She looked like a princess to me. On the contrary, I looked like a brown-coloured beggar having ugly rickshaw-puller hands with skin peeling a bit around my unfiled nails. Nonetheless, I made sure she did not get a hint of my views on us. In fact, I behaved as if I was a confident, handsome prince who had girls queuing up to have him as their boyfriend.

Though I did not notice her eyes slipping on to my clothes, she knew I was wearing local brands; expensive, but still local. Without commenting on my clothes (and embarrassing me), she started shopping for me – branded jeans, branded t-shirt and branded shoes. Obviously, I did not let her pay for any of these things; that would have been very cheap of me. In a couple of hours, she transformed me into a 'brand' new Abby.

After our shopping, we had pizza for lunch. She had the pizza using a fork and a knife in the classiest way possible whereas I ate it using my bare hands because I was more comfortable that way. What people thought did not matter to me. I always told myself, "I set the rules for my life, the people around don't." Saying this to myself always eased the situation for me in social gatherings and meetings.

I was impressed by the way Myra talked in fluent English, the way she carried herself, the way she walked, the way she ate; everything was perfect. Anyone would have loved to have her as his girlfriend. But I still wanted to let go of her. I had been so shattered emotionally in my first relationship that I was not ready for a second one, however good the girl was. To tell you the truth, I was afraid of a break-up. I had survived the first break-up due to my anger towards Shalini. I was not sure whether or not I would be able to cope with a broken heart a second time, if at all a break-up happened. So, I did not want to get into this relationship thing.

We then stepped out of the mall and decided to take a walk on the back-road of the mall, which was neither too crowded nor too isolated. We talked about our respective families and the equations we shared with them. And then came the most relevant topic – boyfriend and girlfriend.

"Do you have a boyfriend?" I asked.

"No. Why?" she asked.

"Just like that."

"Do you have a girlfriend?"

"No. But I have had multiple affairs, out of which only one was close to my heart. Others were short-lived, online flings."

"Then why are you saying 'No'?"

"I am not seeing anyone currently. So, 'no' is technically the correct answer. How come you don't have a boyfriend?"

"I don't know."

"Have you had any serious relationship?"

"Not really. I have had friends who were boys. I still have many, but none of them is or has been my boyfriend in the real sense of the word. All these guys have proposed to me at different points in time, but I have turned them all down."

"Turned them down? All of them? Why? They were not good looking?"

"Looks are important, but I see the entire package, which includes education, intelligence, family background and, of course, caste."

"Caste??? Are you kidding me? Don't tell me you are so ancient in your thinking."

"It is not about being ancient. Every caste has its own qualities. Kayasthas are intelligent and stress a lot on education. I want my kids to focus on education too. If I marry a Punjabi or a Gujarati, he would probably want our kids to get into some business rather than get proper education and a job, and that will not be aligned with my objectives."

"I know where all this is coming from. Your parents must be strict about marrying in the same caste, which is why you have cooked up such stupid arguments to console yourself."

"Whatever the reason, I will not marry outside my caste."

"Ok."

"You have some spicy story up in your head. Tell me about that serious relationship you had."

"Why do you want to know that? She is my past and I do not want to talk about her."

"Please tell me. I want to know. Why did you dump her?"

"I did not dump her, she dumped me."

"What? Why? When? How? Tell me."

I recounted my entire story to her and told her the reason why Shalini broke up with me.

"What? That is a stupid reason. She obviously did not love you. Otherwise, she would have fought for you. She must have found someone better looking than you. I think you should be thankful to her because she saved you by not marrying you. You should not marry the person who you love, but the person who loves you. However banal this statement may sound, it is true," she said.

"I will ask her why she left me, if I ever get to meet her. As of now, she is out of my life and there is no chance she is coming back into it as a friend or anything else. I will not accept her even if she is the last woman on earth," I said to redeem a bit of my self-respect.

"My god! You look so calm and composed from the outside, but there is so much anger inside. You sure are very hurt with what she did. Is she there on Orkut? And is she married? Are you guys in touch?"

"Yes, she added me on Orkut about a month ago. She is married now. We have chatted on messenger a couple of times, but the interactions were very, very formal. Why do you ask so many questions? Are you also a lawyer?"

"I am Sherlock Holmes – the detective. I like getting to the bottom of things."

"Ok Ms Sherlock Holmes, request you to keep whatever I have told you, only to yourself. Nobody knows that Shalini had dumped me. It was a little embarrassing for me to tell people the truth. So, I told everyone that she was forcibly married to someone else and we had to break up."

"You can trust me on that. Hats off to you, man! It takes a lot of courage to accept the rejection and then tell another girl the truth about being dumped. You could have easily lied to me about it."

"Thank you. People who lie are cowards because they are scared of something or the other. I don't need to lie because I am not scared of anything."

"One last question – will you marry her if she comes back to you?"

"Once a girl is out of my life, she is out forever. I don't look back."

"You are a good guy, Abby. I like you."

"Not as good as you think. The relationship with Shalini taught me to be practical and selfish. Myra, don't get me wrong. You are a wonderful and an innocent girl. I don't want to hurt you. So, please do not get sentimental. We will be friends, just friends."

"I am sure I will not get senti on you. You make sure you don't fall for me. Each guy who has been my friend has proposed to me. So keep a regular check on your feelings, sir."

"Sure ma'am. What time are you supposed to get home?"

"Oh my god! It is 7 p.m. already. I have been out for more than eight hours. Talking to you, I did not realize how quickly time passed."

"Time and distance. We must have walked about five kilometres easily. How will you go? Should I drop you on my bike?"

"Yeah, please. But drop me at least a hundred metres away from my building. I don't want my Dad or any of my neighbours to see me with you on a bike."

"Does your Dad know you have come to meet me?"

"No, I did not tell Dad because he is one of those 'Hitler Dads' but I told Mom that I was going to meet you. She knows about you because I tell her everything. I hope she manages the situation."

I dropped her home on my bike and left for mine. During the forty-five minutes I took to reach home, I kept thinking about Myra. Even I had not realized how time passed so quickly. We had kept talking and talking. There was never a dull moment with her.

After reaching home, I messaged Myra to check if everything was fine at her end, but did not get an instant reply, like I used to. I sent her a couple of more messages to call me back as soon as she read my messages, but to no avail. I usually never got tensed, but if somebody I cared for was in trouble and it was beyond my control to help her/him, I got stressed up. This was exactly what was happening. I started praying to god for Myra's well-being and tried to convince myself that she might have got busy with something or she might have put her phone on silent or on charging in some other room. In the couple of flings I had had after Shalini, I had never got this tensed about any of my girlfriends.

"Why are you so worried about Myra? I have seen you this restless only when you were with Shalini. I hope you are not falling for her," the inner Abby stumped me with his question.

"I don't know yaar. Maybe… I mean I like her, but I seriously don't want to get into this love drama again. We can be friends though. And can you please stop bringing Shalini up every time? Can't you just forget that girl?"

"Ok, ok! Coming back to Myra, *ek ladka aur ek ladki, kabhi dost nahi ho sakte*. A girl and a boy can never be just friends, you know."

"I know this Bollywood dialogue makes a lot of sense. I think it is time to end things with Myra then. I will talk to her about this when we meet next. But right now, all I want is a message or a call from her confirming that she is fine."

"Everything will be fine. Don't worry. Myra is a good human being and nothing bad can happen to good people."

I was so tensed about Myra that I did not even feel like having my dinner. I finally received a call from her at about 1 a.m.

"Hi Abby, I am fine. Don't worry," Myra said in a weak voice, the kind of voice we have after crying a lot.

"Myra, your voice is not normal. Are you ok?" I replied.

"Yeah! I told you na, everything is fine. I could not call you or reply to your messages earlier because my phone was on silent and I did not know you had messaged."

"I know you are addicted to your phone. It is not possible that you didn't see my messages. I need to know what happened Myra," I ordered.

"Dad hit me," she said and started crying.

"What? For being late?"

"No. When I returned home, everything seemed normal. Dad looked a little annoyed with me, but he did not say anything. I switched on the computer to email you. When I was writing the email, my elder sister who works in Pune and has come home for the weekend, wanted to use the computer. When I refused, she complained to Dad. He barged into my room and started punching and kicking me. He even got a knife from the kitchen to kill me, but my Mom intervened and pushed him aside."

"I cannot believe it! I want to talk to your Dad. Give me his number."

"Are you mad? What will you tell him?"

"I will tell him that he should know his limits. And next time he thinks of doing such a thing, he should keep me in mind," I said enraged.

"Let it be! He has been like this since our childhood. As it is, I have to get married in a few years and leave this home forever."

"Where did you get hurt Myra?"

"On my face and tummy. They are hurting badly."

"Can I come and see you right now? Is there a possibility?"

"I am not sure. What if I sneak out to meet you and Dad wakes up?"

"Let him wake up. I will not let him touch you, trust me."

"It is ok Abby. We will meet later. I will go off to sleep now."

"Myra, I am coming. I don't know why, but I have to see you. I will call when I reach. Meet me for a couple of minutes, please. If you do not meet me, I will keep waiting outside your building until you meet me. I don't care if I have to wait until tomorrow morning or afternoon," I said and disconnected the call before she could respond.

I reached Myra's place and called her downstairs.

"My god Abby, are you seriously here? Please stop kidding me."

"Yes, I am here. Come down now."

"I am scared. What will I tell Dad if he wakes up and does not find me at home?"

"Why will he look for you so late at night? After what he did to you today, he would least expect you to do such a daring thing. You lock the main door and come. If he catches you entering the house, tell him you were right outside the door talking to one of your building friends. Also call up one such friend right now and brief her on what she has to say if your Dad calls her up."

"Wait a moment! I think Smriti is awake as I can see her bedroom light still on from my window. I will call her first and then leave the house."

"No problem. I will wait. Where is your sister?"

"She is sleeping with Mom and Dad."

"If she wakes up and looks for you, the excuse still remains the same, ok?"

"Yes."

Myra came down after talking to Smriti. The beautiful and cheerful face of the cute girl I had dropped off in the evening was swollen with blue and black injury marks. I was furious. I wanted to go to her home and talk to her Dad to make him feel ashamed of his unmanly and unfatherly act. As I held her face between my palms, tears welled up in her eyes and in mine too.

"Ah! It is hurting," she said and removed my hands.

"Myra, I came here to tell you that you should not take anyone's shit. What you went through tonight, you should never go through it again. Next time your Dad or anyone tries to hit you, you tell him with authority that he has no right to do so."

"Thanks for being there, Abby. You can't imagine what it means to me."

"Anytime Myra. Now go back and sleep. Don't forget to take a painkiller. My heart aches to see you in so much pain."

"I have taken a painkiller already."

She looked up and continued, "You are a friend I could kill to have, Abby. Thanks once again. Message me once you reach home."

"I will. Bye, take care."

"You too. Bye."

As the cyclone of anger inside me abated, the inner Abby surfaced again to talk to me.

"Abby, I think you are getting emotionally involved now. If you delay your vanishing act from her life any further, she will be hurt irreversibly for life and the emotional pain due to it will be worse than the physical pain she is currently battling. Remember how Shalini hurt you emotionally and you still haven't got over that trauma," the inner Abby said to me while I was trying hard to sleep.

"I cannot agree more with you. However, I cannot just vanish. She is a kind soul and she deserves to know that I am going away from her life. I will talk to her tomorrow," I said and slept off.

"Good morning, Myra. How are you feeling now?" I called her the next morning.

"I am better. I bunked office today because I couldn't go to office with a swollen face. What about you? In office?" she said.

"I will leave for office a little late today. I am feeling a little tired."

"I am so sorry Abby. It is all because of me."

"You don't need to be sorry. Whatever I told you last night, keep it with you throughout your life, whether or not I am there with you."

"Is there a chance you will not be with me?"

"You never know Myra. I mean, life is unpredictable."

"Are you planning to leave me?" Myra hit the nail on the head.

"You are a genuine person and I don't want to hurt you. But…"

"Abby, if your only objective was to make me fall for you, let me tell you that you have achieved your objective. You are free to go," she said in a voice choked with emotions.

"Myra, yaar… that was not my objective," I said.

"I will talk to you later. Bye," she said and disconnected before I could say anything else. I was glad she disconnected because I did not have anything worthwhile to say.

There was no doubt that as a person, she was much better than me. I was a little sad because I did have some liking for her, but thanks to Shalini's betrayal, I knew I could easily get over this break-up and delete her from my memory.

8

January 2007 – March 2007
Mumbai/ Patna

I was at a crucial juncture in my life. Myra had indirectly proposed to me and I had to decide whether to board the relationship train with her or not. She was never interested in frivolous relationships. So, her proposition was for marriage, not for dating; whatever I decided would be the decision of a lifetime. As always, I started discussing things with my mentor, the inner Abby.

"I am usually very clear about what I want in my life. But right now, I have to admit I am confused. What should I do? Should I say yes and give this relationship a try? Or should I just walk away? Please tell me," I asked the inner Abby.

"See Abby, after your relationship with Shalini, your mind set a rule of not getting into any relationship. This was done to protect your heart from any emotional agony. And you have stuck to this rule until now. But will you abide by it throughout your life? Will you never marry? You will, right? So, you do plan to get into a relationship later. Then, why not now? Myra is a good girl. She is bubbly, hot, cute, intelligent, and has a great body (I know it matters to you). Above all, she loves you and you are sure of it. What you cannot be sure of, however, is whether or not any other girl you marry in future will love you. I am not saying that the other girl will not love you, but there is always a non-zero probability of her not loving you. Your marriage in that case will be a compromise. You are a great guy, Abby. Any girl will be lucky to have you. If you are anyways going to give this chance to some unknown girl in the future, why not to Myra? And it is not that you don't like her. You do. Actions speak louder than words. You are protective about her and you have feelings for her. It is just that you are running away because you are scared," the inner Abby replied.

"What you say does make sense to me. And yes, I am scared. What if my heart gets hurt again? It might not be able to recover this time."

"Abby, I am your heart. And I am saying that I am ready for it. Go for her!"

"But my mind is advising against it. There is a serious conflict between you two."

"When there is a conflict between your mind and your heart, always listen to your heart, because the heart knows what the mind does not."

The last line by the inner Abby won me over. I called Myra right away.

"Hi Myra, how is your pain now?" I asked.

"How does it matter to you? Why did you call?" Myra answered in a downhearted tone.

"Myra, I am sorry!"

"It is ok Abby. You have the right to decide for yourself. I will be fine. Don't worry."

"I want to meet your parents. When is it possible?" I replied ignoring what she said.

"Why?"

"I want to meet the people who created the most beautiful thing in this world."

"I am not in a mood to take your flattery. Let us talk later."

"Myra, listen. I want to marry you."

"But I don't want to marry you."

"And why is that?"

"Because you don't care for me. You don't love me. You were passing your time with me."

"My time is very precious, Myra. I don't waste it on anyone I don't care for. I care for you. I realized it last night when your pain made me restless. I have been trying to evade my feelings for you, but I can't do that anymore. I like you and I want to marry you. Now, will Princess Myra make Abby her slave for life and give him the opportunity to serve her?" I proposed.

Though I had become too dominating a man to be a slave to anyone, I was willing to make an exception for Myra, the girl I had decided to marry. It was funny how I was ready to break up with her until a few hours ago, but was now proposing to her for marriage.

"Yes slave Abby, Princess Myra will marry you. But there is one condition – our parents should agree to it. If either of our parents say no, I will not marry you."

"You leave that to me. I will handle your parents and mine. You just relax and enjoy the show."

"That is fine, but I will need to introduce you to my parents. How will I do that?" Myra asked.

"Ask your parents that if you select a guy who is educated, working and of the same caste for your marriage, will they meet him? They will hopefully agree. You can then call me over to your place."

"You have guts! You are not scared of meeting my parents alone? Normally boys start getting loose motions at the thought of meeting their girlfriend's parents."

"Thanks for the compliment."

"Mom will be a little busy for the next couple of weeks. She is visiting places across the country to meet prospective grooms for my elder sister."

"What about your Dad? Is he there in town? I can meet him, if you want."

"My Dad does not like anybody in this world, and so he will not like you either. I want you to meet my Mom first. If she likes you, we are through with the first stage. She will convince Dad, but only if you impress her enough."

"Point noted. How does 26 January sound for the meeting?"

"Sounds good. Thanks Abby! You are a sweetheart."

"So are you. Take care, Princess Myra."

"When are we meeting next?"

"Let us meet this Saturday. I have a half-day. I can pick you up from your office and we can go out for lunch or something?"

"Sure! I am excited and nervous."

"I can sense that in your voice. Your pain must have vanished by now."

"I don't care about the pain anymore. You made my day."

From that day onwards, my second love story started rolling, and that too at a high speed. We started talking a lot on phone and met mostly on the weekends. And every time I met her, I liked her even more. She was an entertainer and an incorrigible gossiper. Before I could realize, my liking had turned into love. Our mobile bills sky-rocketed and so did our love.

On my birthday, that was usually a low-key affair, she took a leave from office and we spent the entire day together, shopping and eating. She also gifted me a gold ring with her name etched on it. And then arrived the 26th of January – the day I had to meet Myra's Mom.

I reached her place five minutes before time. Myra met me at her building's gate.

"Why are you dressed in jeans and t-shirt? Why didn't you wear formals? You look irresistible in them," she asked as soon as she saw me.

"Oh! I do not have prior experience of such a meeting. I just wore what I was comfortable in," I replied.

"Ok, let it be now. Nervous?" she asked as we got into the elevator.

"You want me to be?" I answered.

"Obviously not. But I am very nervous. All the best Abby."

"Thanks. Where is your Dad, by the way?"

"He has gone out for some work and will be returning late in the evening."

"He went out for work or was sent out for work?" I joked to release the slight nervousness that was building up inside me.

Myra smiled and rang the doorbell while I clutched her ring in my finger as if it was giving me some kind of divine strength. As soon as her Mom opened the door, I smiled and touched her feet for her blessings.

"Pranaam aunty," I said.

"God bless you, beta," she replied.

Theirs was a two BHK apartment, small by Patna's standards, but big by Mumbai's. Myra offered me to sit on a sofa, while her Mom made herself comfortable on the sofa opposite to mine. And then started the questioning – who all were there in my family and what they did for a living, which place did my ancestors belong to, what was my educational background, what was my job profile, how much did I earn each month, what were my future plans, etc. I answered each of her questions patiently and with a smile. And then came the final two questions, my answers to which won her over.

"Beta, do your parents know about Myra and that you have come to meet me?" she asked.

"No aunty. I have not told them yet. You know how it is in our society. People expect the girl's parents to approach the boy's parents for marriage. Then the boy's family meets the girl and accepts or rejects her. But I believe in equality. So, I came here first without any ego so that you can meet me and take a call on me. If you like me, I will talk to my parents and call them here to meet Myra. You can then come to our house in Patna to discuss the marriage formalities. If you reject me, there is no point telling them about Myra. Both Myra and I have decided that we will not marry if any of our parents do not agree to it."

Myra's Mom did not say anything in response to my answer, but her smile said it all.

"You must be aware that the girl's side has to offer *tilak* (term used to legalize dowry) to the boy's family. What are your expectations? Do not take me otherwise. I am asking you this because Myra's father is a banker with modest earnings and we have four daughters. Two of them are already married, and our third daughter, Sushma is still to get married before we can think of Myra. Grooms with your kind of qualifications usually ask for more than a crore rupees as tilak. We might not be able to afford you."

"Aunty, *dahej to humein dena chahiye* (we should be giving you dowry) because you are giving your precious daughter to us. I don't want anything and I know my parents will not expect anything from you either. I am confident of my capabilities. Whatever I want, I will buy with my money. You just have to give me your daughter."

"Myra, you have made a great choice. I like him. Abby beta, you have a green signal from my side. You can tell your parents about Myra."

"Thank you aunty."

"One more thing. Myra can get married only after Sushma's marriage because there could be problems fixing Sushma's marriage if Myra gets married before her."

"Not a problem. Even I have an elder brother. Myra and I can get married after both the marriages."

"Thanks for understanding, beta."

After the 'interview' and an elaborate lunch that had been prepared especially for me, it was time to leave.

"Pranaam Mummy." I called her 'Mummy' this time instead of aunty, and this floored her. She had four daughters and when I called her 'Mummy', she felt she had got the son she always wanted.

"*Hamesha khush rahiye*, beta (always be happy son). When your parents come, do let me know. I will meet them if they want," she said.

"Sure, Mummy."

Myra came downstairs with me to the building gate to see me off. "You are the best Abby! I am so, so happy. I love you," she said.

"I love you too, Princess. You deserve to be the happiest and I will do anything for that. A-N-Y-T-H-I-N-G," I said.

"I feel blessed. Ride your bike safely and at normal speed. And also let me know when we are meeting next."

"Before that, I need to talk to my parents about you."

"Now, it will be my turn to face your parents. I am nervous."

"Don't be. I will handle my parents. You take care, bye."

"Bye, take care."

The pressure was still on me, not on Myra. I had to tell my parents about Myra and ask them to visit Mumbai before I left in the mid of February for Patna and then to Hyderabad in April for my MBA. I called my Mom as soon as I reached home.

"Hello Mom, how are you?" I asked.

"I am good. I was just browsing through our old pictures. Time has passed so quickly," she replied.

"You browse through the old pictures and then keep crying all day. Why don't you come to Mumbai for a few days?"

"I want to come, but you know how your Dad is, a typical professor. He will not take a single leave from the university. And he has his book-writing that he is perennially busy with."

"Dad will never change."

"When are you getting relieved from office? When are you coming to Patna? What are your plans?"

"I am getting relieved from my office on 13 February and will be coming to Patna on 17 February. So, there are still about three weeks to go. I have to leave for ISB in April. Listen Mom, plan a trip to Mumbai around 13 February. I can take you to Shirdi, where you have always wanted to go, but have never got the opportunity. We can leave for Patna together on 17th."

"Really, you will take me to Shirdi?"

"Of course, I will."

"Let me ask your Dad first. I will confirm by tonight."

"Ok. One more thing Mom."

"What?"

"I want you to meet a girl," I said shamelessly.

"What? Which girl? Which caste is she? What does she do? What does her father do?" Mom barraged me with questions.

"Myra belongs to our caste. She is well-educated and is working at a pharmaceutical company. Her father is a banker and her mother was a lecturer at Patna, but is now a housewife. They stayed in Patna until seven years ago and then shifted to Mumbai."

"Where did you meet her?"

"Where I met her is not that relevant. You come to Mumbai and meet her. If you like her, only then will I marry her."

"Book my tickets right away. For Shirdi, I had to ask your Dad, but for something as important as Myra, I have to come. Your Dad can be on his own for a few days."

"Thank you Mom. I will book the tickets and inform you. Take care. Bye."

I booked her flight for 14 February because the tickets were the cheapest on that date, not realizing that it was Valentine's Day and Myra would be expecting to see me after her office. Thankfully, the flight's arrival was at 7 p.m. So, I had a small window of time to spend with her.

I called up Myra and updated her on Mom's Mumbai visit to increase her levels of excitement and nervousness. In the blink of an eye, it was 14 February. I had already wished Myra at midnight, but it was our first Valentine's Day and I wanted it to be something special, beyond just meeting, eating and shopping.

The proposal episode had already happened between us, but that was over the phone. To formally propose to her face to face on Valentine's Day, I thought of an out-of-the-box plan. To execute the plan, I asked Raj to help, for which he readily agreed. After lunch that day, I left for Shopper's Stop at Inorbit mall and bought a sparkling diamond ring for her.

"Hi Abby, Happy Valentine's Day once again," Myra called and wished me.

"Thank you sweetheart. Wish you a Happy Valentine's Day too," I replied.

"Where are you?"

"I am at Inorbit mall."

"What are you doing at Inorbit mall?"

"I was buying a saree for Mom. I am almost done with it. I should be able to reach your office by 5 p.m. to pick you up. I hope you will be free by that time."

"Oh! I left office early today and have just reached home."

"Home?"

"Arre, we have to receive Mom at the airport na?" Her use of the word 'Mom' for my mother made me feel like kissing her.

"You will come with me to receive Mom? I am not too sure about that."

"But I am. Her flight is landing at 7, right?"

"Yeah."

"It is 4.15 right now. You pick me up from my building at 6.15 sharp."

"Can't you meet me before that?" I said to save my proposition plan from getting ruined. I needed some time to propose to her, I couldn't just do it in haste and spoil the experience.

"Sorry Abby, it will not be possible. I don't have much time; I need to get ready."

"But why do you need two hours to get ready? Just wear any Indian outfit, wash your face, put eyeliner, wear some perfume and you are good to go."

"Girls need time to get ready Abby. Get used to it."

"Yaar! See you at 6.15 then."

I was left with no option but to propose on our way to the airport. I called up Raj and updated him on the new timing for the execution of my plan. Like every Indian, he still had to get a few things done at the eleventh hour. So, instead of getting irritated, he thanked me for giving him some extra time.

By 6.10 p.m., I was at Myra's building waiting in an auto-rickshaw. Few metres behind my auto-rickshaw were four bikes, each with two of my colleagues/friends, including Raj. Everything was set. I called up Myra and asked her to come down.

She looked absolutely stunning in a tight-fitting, figure-revealing black ethnic suit. She seemed like a sparkling diamond wrapped in black, shining from wherever it could (hands, face and neck). Sometimes, traditional Indian dresses arouse you more than western ones, and this was one of those occasions for me.

On the other hand, I was casually dressed in jeans, t-shirt and shoes, all of them gifted by Myra. On my lap, I was carrying a thin jacket; its pocket had the diamond ring with which I had to propose.

We started our journey towards the airport. Without wasting a minute, I slowly tried to take out the ring, but it got stuck in the jacket's pocket. I was still trying to take the ring out when Myra noticed my hands moving under the jacket near my crotch.

"*Kya hua? Khujli ho rahi hai wahan*? (What happened? Is it itching there?)" Myra said and started laughing, embarrassing me to the core. Thank god, she didn't say I was trying to pleasure myself with her beside me.

"You don't have a filter, do you? See that you don't say such things in front of Mom," I said.

"You are right, I don't have a filter. Whatever comes to my mind, I just blurt it out. People who have a filter are dangerous because such people can pretend to be your best friend, but in real, they could be your worst enemy. On the contrary, people who do not have a filter have clean hearts. They will never lie or pretend, and you can blindly trust them."

"Thank you for the *gyaan,* ma'am," I said and made a note of this very important and relevant point she had made.

After enough of 'khujli' on my crotch, I finally got hold of the ring. With my other hand, I gave a missed call to Raj to get things rolling.

On each of the four bikes, the pillion rider was sitting facing the traffic behind, with his back against the rider's back and was carrying a board with something written on it. As the first bike slowly overtook our auto-rickshaw, I drew Myra's attention to it. The pillion rider's board read, "Will". The second bike zoomed past us with the pillion rider's board reading, "You". Then came the third bike with the board, "Marry". And finally, the last bike went past us with the board, "Me?"

"Perfect," I exclaimed. As soon as Myra read the last board, I presented the ring to her and asked in Bhojpuri, "*Humra se shaadi karboo*? (Will you marry me?)".

With her open mouth covered with her palms and her big, beautiful eyes filled with tears of joy, she replied, "Yes, I will."

I slid the ring into her finger and the entire proposal scene was sealed on the happiest note.

We reached the airport on time. When Mom came out, she saw Myra standing beside me and understood she was the girl I wanted her to meet.

"Pranaam Ma," Myra said touching Mom's feet.

"*Khush raho* (be happy)," Mom replied with a smile, analyzing Myra's looks with her critical eyes.

When we sat in the cab, I made Myra sit with Mom on the rear seat while I sat in the front. Mom asked Myra about her parents and other general stuff.

Mom's plan was to stay at my favourite cousin, Neetu di's place. Neetu di had recently shifted to Mumbai with Ajay jiju and their kid, Ritwik. For some unknown reason, I was very close to them. If I had to call anyone in this world at 4 a.m. and expect any kind of help or support, it would be them. It was a given that I wanted Myra to meet them as well before our marriage.

In an hour's time, we reached Neetu di's place where they were waiting to receive Mom and Myra. There was meet and greet at the door, and I introduced Myra to them.

"Great choice Abby!" Jiju exclaimed on meeting Myra. Neetu di's reaction was similar.

During dinner, Myra behaved like a *sanskaari, aagyakaari bahu* (cultured, obedient daughter-in-law) and helped Neetu di serve dinner to everyone. I don't know about Mom, but I was impressed. Myra with her vivacious and bubbly nature replaced me as the favourite of Neetu di's family on that day itself. This thing did not sting me because I wanted her to fit so nicely in my family that she became everyone's favourite.

After dinner, Mummy (Myra's mother) came to pick Myra up. Mom met Mummy and invited her to our Patna house to discuss the way forward.

The next morning, Mom and I left for Shirdi. On our way to Shirdi, I asked Mom her opinion on Myra.

"*Theek hai* (she is fine). She is a little short for you," she said.

"If you do not like her, I will not marry her."

"You have made a choice of your life partner and I will support you in it. In such a short meeting, one cannot find out the true nature of a girl. Since you have spent time with her, I am trusting you for that part. I am fine with the marriage, but the *kundlis* (horoscopes) should match. And one more thing, the marriage can happen only after your elder brother's marriage."

"I am fine with that," I agreed to her harmless conditions.

Myra called me when I was in Shirdi to ask what Mom thought about her. I told her that Mom thought she looked beautiful and that she really liked her. Had I told her Mom's actual views, two things would have happened. One, Myra would have felt bad and sad. Two, Myra would have developed negative feelings for Mom. With one lie, I successfully brushed aside both the issues.

We returned from Shirdi the next day in the evening. It was 16 February and I had to leave Mumbai the next day. Though I was enervated, without a minute of rest, I rushed to meet Myra. When I reached Myra's building, she was already waiting for me outside the building gate.

"Hi would-be Mrs Myra Kartik Chandra, congratulations!" I said.

"Thank you," she blushed.

"How was the trip?" she continued.

"The trip was good," I replied.

"So, what time is your flight tomorrow?"

"9 a.m. Will you come to see me off?

"Of course, I will. I wish I could come along with you all the way to Patna. I want to be with you Abby, all the time. I don't know how I am going to live without you," she said in a feeble voice.

"Don't think about the time we spent together. It will make you sad. Think about the time we are going to spend together in future. I will be staying at Patna for over a month. Why don't you come to Patna with Mummy before I leave for ISB?" I said to lift her mood up.

"That goes without saying. I am coming to Patna to meet you. I will discuss with Mummy and book my tickets at once."

"That's like my good girl."

"I will miss you, Abby."

"I will miss you too Myra. Will see you super soon in Patna and then we will go to your school to eat your favourite *panipuri*," I said and noticed a faint smile appear on her face.

I continued, "Two more things before I leave. One, never think you are alone. I am always there with you. If you get too restless missing me, know that I will just be a call away. You give me a call and I will be standing next to you within twenty-four hours. Two, make it clear to everyone that I will not spare him if he hurts you in any way. If you cry due to anyone, I will make that person pay for it."

"I cannot hug you here in public for obvious reasons. But if you continue your dialogue-*baazi* like this, I will hug you and then kiss you without bothering about the people around," she told me sweetly.

"You are a sweetheart. Take care Myra, I love you."

"I love you too. Take care, bye."

I gave her a sideways hug and we parted. Obviously I was sad, very sad, though I knew I was going to see her in Patna very soon. I also knew that the day I would want to meet her as badly as I wanted to breathe, nothing could stop me from taking the next flight to Mumbai. But I was still feeling downhearted. I requested her not to come to drop us off at the airport because if she came, I would not be able to control my tears. Nobody had seen me cry in the past few years, not even me. Love had finally been successful in casting its shadow on me again, slowly turning me into the old emotional Abby. Despite my request, she did come to see us off. I somehow managed to control my tears, but left Mumbai with a very heavy heart.

Talking to Myra over the phone multiple times during the day and for long hours at night did not let either of us miss the other a lot. Meanwhile, our horoscopes had already been checked for a match and the score was an awesome thirty-four out of thirty-six. Even the planets were strongly in our favour. There was nothing that could stop us from getting married and producing a dozen babies (yes, a cricket team of children is what our horoscopes predicted).

At Patna, my home was not an apartment; it was a three-storied bungalow with eleven bedrooms, huge balconies and sprawling lawns on two sides of it. The property was guarded by eight security guards, including two gunmen. When Myra and Mummy visited my Patna home in the first week of March and saw all of this, it left them impressed. Hitler Dad (Myra's Dad) could not come because he was apparently busy with his office work. Both Mom and Dad met Mummy and Myra very cordially, with no arrogance. Mummy was full of admiration for Dad because he was very simple and down to earth, despite his celebrity status. During their conversation, many common contacts sprung up, bringing relief to either of the families about the family background of the other.

While our parents were busy talking after lunch, I showed Myra my room.

"Wow! I am so excited. This is going to be my room. It is so huge and there is so much scope for decoration. You need to buy pillows, just two won't be enough. You also need to get some soft toys. Get the dull green color of the walls changed to something brighter...," she continued showcasing her interior designing skills, while I kept soaking in her mesmerizing beauty with my big, wide frog eyes.

The next day, I took her around Patna in my Dad's car. We visited her school, had her school's trademark panipuri and met her teachers who recognized her instantly. Then, we went to the house she stayed in during her school days and noticed that it had converted into a playschool. She got nostalgic and started telling me her childhood stories. To listen to her stories and spend some quality time together, I parked my car in front of her old house. While she was excitedly telling me her stories, I held her hand gently between mine. Her stories faded from her lips when she looked into my eyes, which conveyed my request for a kiss. Like an obedient girl, she complied and we kissed, not in that lecherous tongue-eating way, but in a soft, 'cultured' way.

"I am leaving for Mumbai tomorrow. When will we meet next?" she said in an innocent, sweet voice which was followed by tears.

"Do not spoil the moment we just had, Myra. Be happy that everything worked out so smoothly for us. Thank god and our parents for being so kind. The way you and I met accidentally and the way things fell in place after that, is nothing short of a miracle. I have started believing in destiny now. We were destined to meet because we were made for each other. I am so happy to have found my soulmate.

"Don't be sad, for this separation is just a phase and will pass very soon. We can anyways keep talking day and night on the phone until then. And remember, I will always be a call away. You call me and ask me to come to Mumbai, I will reach Mumbai from wherever I am in no time. I am not saying this for the heck of it. You can try me," I said.

"Thank you Abby. You made it so smooth. I really didn't have to do anything. I just watched the show while you performed. I love you, more than anything else in this world," she said.

"I am the hero of my story, sweetheart." I winked at her and hugged her tight, transforming her low-spirited face into a cheerful one.

"You are the hero of my story too!" she replied in a cute but emotionally loaded voice.

Myra left for Mumbai the next day and I left for ISB Hyderabad the next month, armed with her kiss that had fuelled me for the rough road ahead at ISB.

9

April 2007 – June 2008
Hyderabad

The MBA (Post Graduate Program in Management) at ISB was a one-year course. Since this was a two-year normal MBA course condensed into one, it was obviously very hectic and rigorous. There were a total of eight terms of approximately six-week duration each. There were examinations at the end of each term after which there was a week-long term break.

The course started rolling at breakneck speed. At twenty-three years of age, I was the youngest in my batch at ISB. During the first week of lectures, I could not understand most of the things and was under a lot of stress. I kept Myra uninformed about my tensions because I had a good reason for it. Love gives you the strength and confidence to face challenges in life. When you feel low, you always have someone who will patiently listen to you. But at the same time, love also makes you weak because every time you are caught up in a difficult situation, you have someone to run away to and feel comfortable, instead of being strong and fighting out the situation. One is usually stronger and better in life when he knows he doesn't have an emotional cushion to protect him against a fall. So, I never told Myra about what I faced at ISB until I graduated from there because I wanted to battle things out on my own. After all, everyone has to fight his own battle in life.

I had plans of leaving for Mumbai the night my Term 1 examinations ended, but severe diarrhea throughout my examinations made me cancel my tickets. Hearing about my condition, Mom decided to come to Hyderabad the next morning to take care of me. But now, Myra was there to take that burden off her. Myra told Mom that she would travel to Hyderabad to take care of me and that she needn't worry. Though she told Mummy the actual reason for her Hyderabad trip, she told Hitler Dad that she was leaving for an official trip to Pune, because he would have never allowed her to stay alone with me anywhere in the world.

Myra reached ISB the next afternoon and was by my side like a dutiful wife (would-be wife, to be precise) feeding me, putting me to sleep with my head in her lap and catering to all my other needs. I felt so lucky to have met such a caring girl.

The interesting part of her stay was that she stayed in my room and we slept on the same bed sharing the same pillow. We hugged each other and slept during nights and afternoons. I noticed she always, even in the dead of night, smelled of Davidoff Cool Water perfume making me wonder if that perfume was made out of her perspiration. I loved that smell so much that I could fall in love with any girl who used that perfume.

Coming to the non-interesting part, we did not even make out, leave aside having sex. It could be because I was not well or because I was decent enough to not cross the line. Throughout the four days that she stayed with me, she kept talking relentlessly. She told me many stories of her childhood, each interesting in its own way. Like before, neither of us got bored even for a second in the company of the other. We sure were made for each other.

The four golden days vanished in a snap of my fingers. At the airport, when she was about to go inside, I gave my parting speech.

"Thanks for coming here and taking care of me Myra, without thinking a bit about your own job. I will never forget this. I am so happy I am going to marry you. As I have told you before, know that I am only a call away. Hyderabad is better connected to Mumbai than Patna. I can reach your place within a few hours; you just have to give me a call. Now go, otherwise you will miss your flight. I love you. Happy journey!"

"You have your studies to keep you busy but I get a lot of free time, and during those times, your memories flash and make me cry. I am not as strong as you are. I love you a lot Abby and I can't live without you," she said with the tears in her eyes about to jump onto her cheeks.

Her reply was so cute that I could not help but hug her and kiss her on the lips. She was a simple, shy girl who got terribly unsettled because of my public display of affection. Due to the kiss-induced short circuit in her head, she immediately turned around and started heading towards the airport building gate in haste, forgetting to take her luggage trolley along. I had to call out her name a couple of times to get her to come back and take it.

Till I returned to my room, I was calm, composed and strong, but as soon as I entered my room, locked it and turned around, her memories started haunting me. I had a glass of water and started deep breathing to control my tears. I lay down on the bed and buried my face in the pillow to cut off myself from Myra temporarily and get back to normal. But this was like running towards something you actually want to run away from. The pillow and the bed smelled of her and made me burst into tears, something which had not happened in a long, long time. A sharp sting of pain pierced my heart, making me cringe. My throat started hurting and it became increasingly difficult to breathe. There was a sense of emptiness, as if something was missing inside my chest, maybe my heart.

I wanted to take the next flight to Mumbai and be with Myra forever. Love was making me weak. I felt I would not be able to live without Myra even for a second. Who knew, a time would come when I would not be able to live with Myra.

The inner Abby helped me take control of the situation. Myra was expected to call any moment to tell me that she had reached Mumbai and if she came to know that I had been crying, it would have made her life more difficult. So, I mustered all the strength I could to at least sound normal.

"Hi Abby, I have reached Mumbai," Myra called soon after.

"Hey Myra, how was the flight?" I asked feigning I was in a good mood.

"Very bad. I kept crying throughout the flight," she said.

"Myra, you have to be strong. Think about the next time we will meet. It is just a month away and the month will pass in the blink of an eye. Keep yourself busy at work until then."

"You have to do well at ISB. Focus on your studies there. I will be fine. Take care. Love you a lot!"

"Same here, Myra. Know that I will be able to focus on my studies only when I am sure that my sweetheart is fine. So, do not cry and be happy."

"I know. Now start preparing for Term 2. Catch up with you later."

"Sure. Take care… I love you the most Myra!" I said and signed off.

Wherever I went – the canteen, the club, the main building, it had memories of the time I had spent with Myra. The situation in my room was even worse because every single piece of furniture in the room reminded me of her. It took me a good three to four days to pull myself out of my sorrow. I was amongst the toppers in Term 1 examinations and that helped me focus back on my studies.

Term 2 was better than Term 1 because I had adjusted to the hectic curriculum, thanks to my quick learning capability and an enviable stamina to study. After Term 2 examinations ended, I left for Mumbai for five days, to be with my love. This time, I dared to stay at her home. I was put up in Myra's room while Myra shifted to her parents' room.

My interaction with Hitler Dad was very limited because he left for office before I woke up in the morning and at night, he slept before Myra and I returned home after partying. I did meet him the night I had reached Mumbai, but we had just exchanged pleasantries. He was not very welcoming of me for obvious reasons – he did not know the kind of person I was, and I was still not married to his daughter. He was also dead against love marriages.

On one of the nights when Mummy and Hitler Dad were asleep, I called Myra to my room and we made out that night, amidst fears of Hitler Dad catching us in the act, red-handed. Had he caught us, he would have killed both of us. That day, I came to know one thing about myself. I had a lot of guts. To stay at your girlfriend's house at night and make out with her with the door of your room open while her parents (more importantly, Hitler Dad) slept in the other room, takes a lot of courage and bravery.

The next day was a Sunday and Hitler Dad was at home. He appeared a little stressed out due to some reason. When I asked Myra about the reason, she told me that it was some loan issue that had been troubling him for the past three years. Eyeing a window of opportunity to interact with him, I worked out a solution for him. The solution left him impressed and broke the ice between us. I also helped him recover some priceless videos and photographs that were trapped in his 'out of order' digital camera for over a year. The tensed equation between Hitler Dad and me finally started to ease.

In the afternoon, when I was about to go out for lunch with Myra, Mummy said that she wanted to talk to me alone. Sensing an unpleasant conversation coming my way that could cause me stress, I thought of facing the situation right then instead of postponing it by a couple of hours.

"Beta, do not take me otherwise, but Myra visited you at Hyderabad last month and now you visited us in Mumbai. In future also, this is going to continue. I am a little concerned about what people around will say because they have seen you coming to our house and staying here. You know how these people are.

They might start maligning Myra and our family. The future is uncertain. What if something goes wrong and you don't marry Myra? Sushma is still to get married. We might have problems in getting both of them married if that happens," she said.

"I understand your point Mummy. Your concerns are totally justified. But I cannot marry Myra till my brother gets married. What else can I do to assure you that I will not leave your daughter?" I said.

"Can I get Myra and your court marriage done?"

"Mummy, I am not like the usual guys who get into frivolous relationships. If I have said that I will marry Myra, I will. Nobody in the world can stop me, except Myra herself. However, since you are her Mom, you are my Mom as well. Take an appointment for our court marriage next month. I will come to Mumbai a day before that and relieve you of your tension," I said.

I was not having a fling with Myra. I was serious about her and would have married her, come what may. The court marriage would not affect anything, except giving me the legal right to take decisions about her life (obviously with her consent) and protect her from anyone, even from her parents.

"Thank you, beta. I am so relieved. I will get the appointment."

I left Mumbai later that night with a heavier heart than ever, with the same feelings I had whenever we had parted with each other earlier. The difference was that this time, memories of me staying at Myra's house haunted her more than they haunted me because she had to stay in that house without me around.

Soon, Term 2 results were out and I remained among the toppers. July 19, in the middle of my Term 3, seemed like an auspicious day to Mummy's Pandit ji and was finalized as the date of our court marriage. On July 18, I reached Mumbai to marry my sweetheart and make her mine forever. Hitler Dad was apparently not informed about it. Even I had not informed Mom and Dad about it because I knew Mom would never agree to it, though it was a harmless thing and held no value for anyone in the long run. They knew I was going to marry Myra anyway.

Myra and I legally married on July 19. It looked a little funny, putting the garland around each other's neck in the court and taking wedding wows. We partied till late that night, eating, drinking and smoking together. Sex was an obvious thing to do to seal the night, but we did nothing beyond making out. I was in a super happy state of mind and so was Myra. We wanted to spend more time together, but I had to return to Hyderabad the next day to get on with my Term 3.

From that day onwards, whenever I visited Mumbai, I used to stay at Myra's place and we used to sleep on the same bed, which made me wonder if Hitler Dad was really in the dark about our court marriage. Another thing was how conveniently Mummy had ignored her strict condition of Myra's marriage happening only after Sushma's. Not one to strain myself over such insignificant issues, I went ahead with the flow.

Term 3 was smooth and I continued the consistency with respect to my grades.

Giving pleasant surprises to whoever I loved always brought joy to me, surprises that often held the person spellbound. One day, in the middle of Term 4, Myra sounded disturbed on the phone. Sensing that she was upset about something, I took the next flight to Mumbai. She was left open-mouthed when she opened the door and saw me. Unsurprisingly, she was ecstatic. She hugged me, kissed me and did not let go of my arm for an hour, thanking me for my unexpected visit which was only to lift her spirits and mood.

Time flew and it was October. The results of Term 4 came out and I made it to the Dean's List (list of students in the top 10% of the batch, academically) of ISB. It was a big achievement, considering the level of my batchmates against whom I was competing. Being a 'Dean's Lister' almost guaranteed a shortlist by most of the companies during placements, and so, was going to be a big advantage for me over 90% of my batchmates.

I was in the middle of my fourth term break which, unlike other week-long term breaks, was ten days long, and was to continue until October 14. I did not tell Myra that I was having my term break. Instead, I told her that my examinations were on. It was her twenty-second birthday (the first one with me) on 11 October and I wanted to give her a surprise visit. Had she known I was having my term break, she would have expected me to come to Mumbai on her birthday. Due to my examination excuse, she was least expecting me to stun her.

On 10 October, I was supposed to reach Mumbai by 11 p.m. and then reach Myra's home forty-five minutes later, right in time to wish her. But my flight got delayed by an hour. I switched off my phone when I sat in the flight and did not switch it on till I reached her home at 12.45 a.m. Forty-five minutes of her birthday had passed and I had not called to wish her. I knew she would be mad at me, and might even be crying. I could have called her from the cab or the airport, but I didn't want her to get any hint of me being on the way to her place.

That would have ruined the special surprise I had in store for the occasion.

I had bought twenty-one gifts for her, one each for every birthday that I had missed since she was born. The gifts were bought according to the age she would have been on each of her birthdays. So, for the first birthday, I had got a rattle; for the second birthday, I had got alphabets and numbers; and so on. I reached her doorstep and with a racing heart, started placing the gifts on the floor year-wise at about one foot distance from each other so as to lead to some end point where I would be sitting as her twenty-second gift. I made sure that the last few gifts reached the stairs and were placed on the same flight of stairs. I sat down on the next flight of stairs so that she would not be able to see me unless she picked up all her twenty-one gifts. On my shirt, I stuck a paper that read,

"I missed your twenty-one birthdays, but not this one."

I rang her doorbell and quickly ran to take my place on the stairs. Nobody opened the door. I rang the bell again and waited on the stairs for her to come. Still, nobody opened the door. I called Mummy and requested her to ask Myra to open the door. I have no idea what was going on in her head, because she herself opened the door. Imagine Mummy picking up all the gifts and reaching me on the stairs. Fortunately, common sense dawned upon her when she saw the gifts and she called Myra. One by one, Myra picked up all her gifts and by the time she reached me, she was in tears. She had never imagined such a surprise even in the best of her dreams. My surprise act bowled over not just her, but her parents, sisters, friends and anyone else who heard about it and won me the title of 'The Surprise King'.

Myra's birthday was spent shopping and partying until late. I left Mumbai a couple of days later to face the most crucial part of my ISB journey – the placements.

Term 5 onwards, the placement scene at ISB started heating up a bit, with representatives from various companies visiting ISB for pre-placement talks.

My regular visits to Mumbai continued until the mid of January. We now had less than a month to go for 14 February, the 'Day 0' (the first day) of placements. Before that, came my birthday on 24 January and I was not even thinking about it.

Since I was busy preparing for my interviews, I made it clear to Myra that I would visit Mumbai only after I got placed. I told her that the placements would start on 21 February, the day they were actually going to end (the placements usually lasted for a week). I told my parents the same thing. I lied to both Myra and my parents because had they known the exact date of the placement week, they would have kept calling me every day during that week to ask whether I got placed or not, thus putting me under unnecessary pressure to secure a job.

On the morning of 24 January, somebody knocked at my door early in the morning when I was still fast asleep. I opened the door with my eyes half closed and saw a very fair, beautiful girl standing there. Thinking it was one of my ISB batchmates who lived in a Quad (ISB's student apartment with four rooms) right above mine, I said 'Hi' and sat back on my bed. When the girl started laughing, I realised it was a familiar voice. It was Myra who had surprised me this time.

When I was done with my lectures that day, she called and asked me to come directly to the Executive Housing (EH) – the guesthouse at ISB. She had booked a room in the EH well in advance, so that both of us could spend the evening together without any disturbance.

In the evening, I cut my birthday cake with Myra. We drank beer and had a lavish dinner in the comfort of our room at the EH. She gifted me a digital camera, something she knew I wanted. The next gift that she gave me was not gained, but lost by both of us. Both of us lost our virginity to each other that night. There could not have been a better *muhurt* (auspicious date and time) for it. That night I realized why people were crazier about sex than any other method of self-satisfaction.

Myra left for Mumbai on 26 January. I did get a little depressed but my focus on the interview preparations overshadowed my depression.

Day 0 arrived. All the biggies like McKinsey, BCG, Oliver Wyman (OW), A. T. Kearney, HUL, Microsoft, etc., were allotted Day 0 slots so that they could hire the best. OW was the most sought after because it was offering one of the highest packages in an international location and every student at ISB wanted to get into it. I was shortlisted for interviews by as many as twelve companies on Day 0 itself. All the companies had multiple rounds of interviews, with elimination in each round. The interviews were gruelling and by the end of the day, I was totally exhausted. I had not even got the time to talk to Myra since morning, leave aside putting any food to my mouth. At night, Myra and I talked for about five minutes during which I told her that I was having a terrible migraine and needed to rest.

Sleep eluded me that night, probably because I was tensed about the results. I had given the final round of interviews of six companies on Day 0 – OW, BCG, Microsoft, HUL, A. T. Kearney and Accenture. Due to lack of time, I had to skip interviews of three companies. The next morning, when I was waiting for my interview with Diamond Management Consulting, I saw people congratulating a couple of students who had been informed about their selection at OW, BCG, etc. The placement memories of IIT started flashing before my eyes. I did not want to go through the same experience again.

In the afternoon, I did not feel like having lunch. I was drowning in depression and needed to motivate myself. I went to the library and switched on my laptop to check the status of my applications to Day 1 companies so that I could plan my options. There were about twenty new emails. The first one was about my final round of interview with Diamond Management Consulting and it was due in the next fifteen minutes. The priority for me was to nail it anyhow and not think about anything else that time. I was about to log out from my email account when the word "Congratulations" in the subject of one of the emails crossed my eyes. The email was from the Placement Cell informing me of my selection at OW. I read the mail again and again in disbelief, with intermittent faint smiles on my face. When reality sunk in, I could not control the drops of tears that rolled down my cheeks.

"You did it Abby, you did it!" I congratulated myself and breathed a sigh of relief. Since I already had a job offer, I immediately pulled out of the placements to make way for other students.

When I received the offer letter from OW, the inner Abby was jumping with joy. Had it got a little more excited, it would have jumped out of my body and I would have been dead. OW offered me a position in Dubai with an annual package of more than a crore rupees, and that too tax-free.

I informed Myra, Mom, Dad, Mummy and Hitler Dad about my placement. All of them were proud of me. Myra was probably the happiest, because it was her childhood dream to settle abroad, which I came to know about much later. Little did she know that I, her hero, would be the villain who would unknowingly shatter her dreams for his own.

This was the best phase of my life. I had the best girl as my wife who loved me more than anything else in the world, and a high-paying job in a city like Dubai. My reputation and popularity reached an all-time high, with my friends increasing at an enormous rate. People gazed at me with longing. Anyone would have killed to be in my shoes. There was free flow of love, some of it belonging to me, but a lot of it belonging to my professional success.

While a lot of people (including me) thought it was already the 'And he lived happily ever after' moment for me, it was actually a '*Picture abhi baaki hai mere dost*' moment. There was more to come.

10

July 2008 – December 2008
Dubai

I was to join OW on 6 July and had my flight to Dubai on 4 July from New Delhi. Mom and Dad came to New Delhi from Patna to see me off. Myra also travelled to New Delhi from Mumbai to spend three days with us before I left for Dubai. She had come despite being down with severe food poisoning that was causing her a terrible stomachache and nausea.

On the first day of her stay, Mom and I were talking to her to distract her from her nausea, when she couldn't control herself and puked. I caught her vomit in my hands. For someone who threw up even at the site or stink of puke, it was a big deal holding the partially digested food in my hands. I was with her all the time, feeding her, taking her to the washroom whenever she wanted to, giving her medicines on time, etc., and ensured she was in a much better position by the time I had to leave for Dubai.

Leaving India was an emotional affair. Mom and Myra kept crying while Dad and I kept consoling them saying that they could visit Dubai or I could come to India anytime they wanted. I also wanted to cry my heart out, but kept my calm to live up to my image of a tough guy. But inside, I felt like I was leaving pieces of myself behind.

At the Dubai airport, I was greeted by a beautiful *Marhaba* (welcome) escort who guided me swiftly through the immigration formalities. Right outside the airport, there was a chauffeur waiting for me to drive me in an Audi through the glittering city of Dubai to a seven-star serviced accommodation in the upscale Dubai Marina, which lit up my sleepy eyes. From a small town like Patna to a flashy city like Dubai, it had been quite a journey.

Soon, my projects started and so did the tours. Staying at the client's site (that was usually out of Dubai) for four days in a week was normal. The fifth day, we had to report at our base office in Dubai. Just in case it excites you, we were always put up in seven-star hotels while at the client's site.

Since my weekends were off, every weekend, I visited Myra in Mumbai for a couple of days or she visited me in Dubai for a week. And whenever we met, I pampered her a lot. Shopping had always been her favourite activity. Earlier, both of us had to think a little about money before buying anything. But now, anything she placed her hands on was literally hers. I bought her everything she wanted – designer shoes and clothes, laptops, high-end mobile phones, etc.

When we were not physically together, we were glued to our phones talking to each other. My average monthly phone bill shot up to the tune of forty thousand rupees. The best thing was, even after spending so much, I could still save enough.

In October, I visited India for a week to be with Myra on her birthday. I had promised her that I would buy her a gold waist chain when I had seen her wearing a silver-plated one before. So, on this birthday, I gifted her one. I gifted both – my Mom and Mummy with similar gold necklaces that became their favourite pieces of jewellery. I wanted to be fair to both my mothers to set an example for Myra. I also took a test drive of the newly launched Honda City car because I wanted to gift both sets of my parents a car each during my next visit in January. I had the money and I wanted to buy the world for my loved ones.

When I returned to Dubai after Myra's birthday, both of us were missing each other terribly.

"Hi Myra, I am missing you a lot," I called her and said.

"Same here. More so because you forgot to take the t-shirt you were wearing yesterday," she replied.

"Oh! You get it washed and keep it with you. You can give it to me when we meet next."

"No, I will not get it washed."

"What? Are you crazy? It must be stinking of my sweat."

"When you love someone, you love everything about that person, even his natural body odor. I will not get your t-shirt washed till it has your smell in it. I am wearing it right now because it makes me feel you are with me all the time."

Such was the limit our love had reached. I nicknamed Myra as *jaan*, meaning life, because she had literally become my life. Love did not define us anymore, we defined love.

Amidst all my happiness, there was one interesting event that was completely unexpected, but immensely satisfying. It was my chance encounter with a familiar face, that of my IIT batchmate – Ashish, who had mocked me for my paltry salary at L&T. ISB was hosting an information session in Dubai and I was one of the speakers, while Ashish was one of the prospective applicants. After the session, he came to me. We exchanged pleasantries, as well as the details about our salary figures. This time, my salary was more than ten times his and I had achieved it within a span of three years, proving beyond doubt as to who was a bigger *chutiya*.

Meanwhile, I did not realize that an 'infection' that had originated in my heart when I was at IIT had now reached my brain – 'Entrepreneurship', my next goal in life.

"You work so hard, day and night. Agreed that you are earning a salary most people can only dream of. But then, what exactly is your aim in life? Do you want to keep taking orders from people who are not as smart as you? Do you want to keep making presentations and business models for someone else to take the credit of? Do you want to keep working to make someone else's dream a reality? What about your dream?" the inner Abby questioned me one night.

"Well, my dream was always to start a company of my own," I replied.

"Then what are you doing here?" the inner Abby asked.

"I am getting myself equipped with professional skills that can help me set up a successful venture," I replied.

"You have attended workshops and have also worked on a few projects. You know you are equipped for entrepreneurship. What are you waiting for?"

"I don't know. Maybe I want to earn some more money to ensure a life of affluence for my family members and myself."

"I guess you are also acting under the social pressure of being in a job. You know that people will respect you more if you have a job. But is that what you really want to do? For how long do you want to keep living your life the way other people want or expect you to? It is time you stop thinking about these people and start living for yourself."

"But I live amongst people. I have to think about them."

"Always remember that in this world, everyone is alone and has to fight his own battle in life. Success is like a sugar cube in your life and these people are like ants gathered around that cube. The moment the sugar cube vanishes from your life, these ants will run helter-skelter to suck up to someone else with a sugar cube. Their love and respect are conditional. So stop thinking about them! Tell me one thing, when you are dying, do you want to tell yourself that you wanted to do something but you did not even attempt it? I don't think so. When you are on your deathbed, these people who you are thinking about, might not even be there by your side. It will only be you. And at that time, you will curse yourself for not having run after your dream. Don't do what others expect you to do; do what you expect yourself to do."

"What about Myra and our parents? What will I tell them? They will not agree to it. How will I convince them?"

"This is your life and you have the right to take decisions for yourself. If they love you, they will understand and support you. My advice is to resign first and then tell them about it because if you ask them for their suggestion, they might try to influence your decision and confuse you further."

"Let me sleep over it and then decide," I replied.

There was immense confusion between my heart and my mind regarding taking the entrepreneurial plunge. So, I went by my rule –

"Whenever there is a confusion between your heart and your mind, listen to your heart because it knows what the mind does not."

Entrepreneurship had the backing of my heart and it could also help me fulfil my dream of living in contentment and abundance. So, I decided to choose a life full of struggles and challenges (entrepreneurship) over a life full of comfort (job). I did not want to be a part of the rat race anymore.

It was not that I did not know what I wanted to start. I wanted to start an educational publishing company. The content that was available to Indian students that time was of inferior quality. There was a huge gap in the market for good quality content and I wanted to fill that gap through books from my publishing company.

I planned a trip to India to face the resistance from my parents, my in-laws and Myra in person, as opposed to facing it over the phone. I informed Myra of my resignation the night I landed in Mumbai. She was obviously taken aback with my decision, but kept mum.

"Abby, Mummy and Dad want to talk to you. They are waiting in the living room," Myra said when I woke up the next morning. She had told Mummy and Hitler Dad about my resignation.

"Yeah, sure," I replied.

"Beta, why are you resigning? You have such a high-paying, reputable job, and that too abroad. Please do not resign," Mummy said.

"Mummy, I want to go after my dreams," I replied.

"But beta, you can also do that side by side, while being in a job," Hitler Dad said.

"If I do two things at the same time, I will screw up both. Entrepreneurship requires focus. So my own company should have the entire share of my mind," I said.

"Kayasthas cannot handle business. They can only work in a job. You won't be able to succeed," Mummy played the caste card.

"That is the most archaic thing I have ever heard. Who did this 'match the following' between castes and the profession they would be successful in? My entrepreneurial success depends on my capabilities, not on my caste," I replied.

"You are not ready to understand, beta. We have already told everyone in our contacts that you are working in Dubai and earning a crore every year. What will we tell them? Our chest that is puffed with pride will shrink with shame," Hitler Dad tried to play the emotional card now.

"Do you care more for the people or me? You people had told me that I am like the son you never had. Will you not support your son in what he is doing?" I countered.

"Of course, we will support you. But what if your venture fails? Nobody will hire you back," Hitler Dad played the failure card.

"Publishing companies are running profitably across the world. If my venture starts inching towards failure, it would mean I did something wrong. So, I will correct my mistake and eventually be successful. For me, the option of failure is not there. If I keep that as an option, chances of my failure will be higher," I played the success card.

"Beta, I know astrology. From what I have studied in your horoscope, you and I are similar in the sense that we are escapists. We run away from challenges. I believe, you are running away from challenges at your job to opt for a comfortable life," Mummy played the astrology card.

"If you think setting up and running one's own company is easy, then I am afraid you are wrong, Mummy. In fact, being in a job is comfortable and non-challenging. I am running towards challenges, not away from them," I replied.

"Nobody wants to marry off their daughter to someone who is not working," Mummy played the Myra card and the threatening card simultaneously.

"In that case, don't marry her off to me till I become successful. By the way, she is already married to me," I said.

"But why publishing, Abby? You will be printing books and selling them. You are so educated and qualified, at least think of some other business," Hitler Dad played the qualification card.

"If I told you I was starting a company like Nestle, would you feel proud of me?" I asked.

"Yes, Nestle is a great company. Start something like that," Hitler Dad replied.

"What does Nestle do? It conducts market surveys, understands the needs and preferences of the customers, designs its products accordingly, manufactures those products and then through a network of distributors and retailers, makes them available to the end consumers. A publishing company is very much like Nestle. The only difference is that the products here, are books. Everything else is similar. Most people think that publishing is a business in which you run a printing press, but that is not true. Printing is the manufacturing of books and it forms only a part of the entire line of work. Now are you comfortable?" I said.

"You should have been a lawyer. Nobody can win an argument against you," Hitler Dad said, signalling the end of my exit interview.

It seemed as if Mummy and Hitler Dad had discussed and prepared an exhaustive list of questions to ask me. I am not sure, but Myra might have helped them prepare it. The positive side of this grilling interview was that it prepared me for my next interview with my parents, who asked me similar questions. They, however, were more supportive.

I returned to Dubai to wrap things up there, and about a month later, returned to India to board the entrepreneurship train which gave me one hell of a roller coaster ride full of victories and failures, happiness and sadness, hope and disappointment, satisfaction and frustration, and a lot of popularity.

11

December 2008 – September 2009
Patna

On 1 December, I left Dubai for good and landed in Mumbai. Sushma's wedding was scheduled on 5 December in Dhanbad and I was expected to attend it. My plan was to attend Sushma's wedding and then head off to Patna to start my own firm.

Hitler Dad had still not softened completely towards me and Sushma's wedding gave me the perfect opportunity to change his attitude. He did not have a son and had to make all the wedding arrangements alone. From the time I landed in Mumbai, I helped him relentlessly in managing the wedding preparations without caring about my meals or anything else, from morning till the dead of night. Just like Shahrukh Khan impressed Amrish Puri in the movie *Dilwale Dulhania Le Jayenge*, I impressed my Hitler Dad. During the wedding, I also made sure I gelled well with all of Myra's relatives (including her sisters), who thought of me as an ideal son-in-law.

After the wedding, Myra left for Mumbai and I returned to Patna to start my publishing company, Eduwiser.

With my hard work, quick learning capacity and headstrong attitude, I kept climbing the ladder of success on the professional front. But on the personal front, my relationship with Myra started going downhill.

Myra was very straight forward in nature. If she felt something was wrong or if she did not like anything about a person or his work, she would say it to his face, without thinking about his feelings. Her tone was inherently loud and she often sounded a little rude while trying to put across her point. However, she had always been polite to me, making me the privileged one. But after my return from Dubai, I noticed a change in Myra's attitude towards me. She had turned rude to me as well. During my monthly visits to Myra in Mumbai, there were multiple occasions when she shouted at me in public for petty issues, leaving me embarrassed. I made it clear to her that she should avoid shouting at me in front of a third person because it made me feel insulted. I needed respect in the relationship, but she didn't care. Until I was in Dubai, I was Myra's priceless possession, but after my return, I had become her discarded possession.

Before I came into Myra's life, she was not allowed to go out after 10 p.m. But after our court marriage, her time restrictions at home had been lifted. Whenever Hitler Dad questioned her on her late night parties, she told him that she had my permission. From my side, I had given her the permission to party because I never liked imposing any kind of restriction on her. She was an independent girl and had full rights to do what she wanted to. But her safety was of prime concern to me. When I used to request her to drink in control and be very cautious while taking drinks at parties (because people could spike her drink), she would fire an acerbic reply, "I am not a kid. Don't tell me what to do." Such replies continued even after she once had to be hospitalized for severe dehydration due to excessive drinking. She was on medication and was not supposed to go overboard with her drinking, but she did and almost suffered a heart attack. I was in Patna at that time and had to rush to Mumbai to be by her side.

To get rid of my newfound irritation for Myra, I made myself busier with work, while Myra got busier partying every night with her friends; friends who were very progressive in their thoughts and activities, if you know what I am talking about. The phrase *Nazar se door, dil se door* (out of sight, out of mind) had proved itself correct in Shalini's case, and it was trying to do the same again.

As our boats started drifting apart in the sea of our relationship, I felt like a helpless spectator. Myra had changed and there were probably multiple reasons for it. One, my decision to return to India to pursue my dreams had shattered her dream of settling abroad after marriage (a dream I did not know mattered more to her than anything else in the world, even her relationship). Two, she was apparently materialistic and with me earning a fraction of what I used to when I was in Dubai, her love and respect for me had reduced. That way she was no different from my other acquaintances who had flocked around me when I was in Dubai, but who vanished when I quit my job.

Three, she had recently been partying a lot with good-looking guys who used to hit on her, making her believe that she could easily get a richer and better-looking guy than me. And four, the frequency of our meetings and our talks on phone had reduced due to my hectic professional life.

Fed up with Myra's rude and indifferent behaviour, I called up Mummy and told her that her daughter was a headache I did not want to take for the rest of my life. I told her that Myra was absolutely out of my control and I needed a divorce. Since nobody knew about the court marriage, it would not have created any problem for Myra in her next marriage. Mummy assured me that she would talk to Myra about it, but I knew Myra would not listen to her and would get further agitated. She had become a rebel and I was responsible for it, because I was the reason she got the freedom she was now misusing. If it were not for our court marriage, both of us would have married different people.

If you want to make a relationship work, at least one person has to keep calm. If both are aggressive, the connecting thread of the relationship wears off very quickly. I wanted to give our relationship a try, and a good one at that, because I wanted it to work. I knew I could control my aggression but Myra could not; whatever she felt, be it anger or excitement, would come out unfiltered and uncontrolled. So, I put my god's gift of patience to test and started preparing for our marriage ceremony (the public marriage) that was due on 12 December, a week after my elder brother's marriage.

12

October 2009 - October 2011
Patna/ Mumbai

Amidst the excitement of our marriage and the thought of living together, Myra and my relationship improved. In October, just before her birthday, she quit her job because the plan after marriage was to settle in New Delhi (since it was a metro with a decent standard of living and was also a hub for publishers) where her company did not have an office. I went to Mumbai to be with her on her birthday and stayed there for a couple of weeks, during which we spent a lot of time together. My physical presence meant absence of her friends from her life for some time, and this helped our relationship recover from its bad phase.

Myra and I had a grand wedding on 12 December at a five-star hotel in Patna. Everything happened as expected, except one thing. During the *vidai* ceremony (in which the bride says bye to her parents and other relatives, and leaves their home to live with the groom), instead of hugging Myra and kissing her, Mummy hugged and kissed me. Myra, on the other hand, was smiling, unlike the usual brides who cry their lungs out during the vidai. In fact, there was no drop of tear from anyone in her family. It was strange, but just went on to imply that Myra and her family were convinced I would take good care of her and she would be happier with me.

I was extremely excited and relieved because Myra and I could stay together now. For almost two years, we had been visiting each other in different cities and were always busy over the phone with each other. So, staying together also meant saving a lot of money on air tickets and phone calls.

After an unforgettable honeymoon in Maldives and Bangkok, I resumed work in January and kept shuttling between different cities with Myra to manage my work. Anyone who has stayed in Mumbai for a few years cannot settle anywhere else in India, and Myra was no exception. She longed to go back to Mumbai. For six months, I kept trying to convince her to settle in New Delhi, but had to finally give in to her wish of moving back to Mumbai.

In July, I bought an apartment in Lokhandwala, Myra's favourite locality because she had stayed there for a long time. Together, we set up our new home with love, care and innocence.

We spent hours talking to each other and strangely enough, never got bored of one another. We did everything together – grocery shopping and cooking, partying, drinking, smoking and gossiping throughout the night. We did not need a third person to entertain us; we were enough for each other. Both of us had similar tastes in movies, TV shows, food, etc. So, there was minimal argument and fighting over things like the TV remote or which food we should order/cook or which movie we should watch, etc.

If you want your marriage to last, your spouse and you should become the best of friends and be very honest with each other. Myra and I were the best buddies. We were so open with each other that I could check out any woman and call her sexy in front of her without worrying about the consequences a normal wife would subject her husband to on doing the same. Even she could check out men in front of me because she had that liberty as well.

Her limited cooking skills did not bother me much, as I was not one of those typical husbands who would sit uselessly on the couch watching TV and demand his favourite dishes to be cooked and served to him by his wife. Instead, I preferred cooking with her and having romantic moments in our kitchen; my favourite one being Myra cooking while I hugged her from behind with my chin on her shoulder. Later, we kept a cook who took care of our meals on all days, except Sundays, when I used to cook Myra's favourite dishes, rajma-chawal or chicken curry-rice.

Myra was a person known for her talkative and outgoing nature, while I was known for my quiet and calm demeanour. However, I was a completely different person when I was with her. I was so talkative with her that she had to literally put her hand on my mouth to get a chance to speak. Not everything I said to her made sense. A lot of it was apparently crap, including the 'Abby's Laws of Life' that I had come up with, the first of which stated that:

"The total measure of each thing in one's entire life is a constant."

For example, the total amount of happiness one would get in his entire life is a constant. If a person has been very happy in his early life, it means he has used up a major chunk of happiness from the total measure of happiness allocated to him for his life. So, he will be left with little happiness for his remaining life. Similarly, the total number of hours one would be awake for in his life is a constant. If he sleeps less, he is using up his 'awake hours' rapidly and so, he will die younger. This also means that he will live longer if he sleeps more.

The same applies to love. I had been short on love in my life until I met Myra. I had a chance of getting love from Shalini, but I got betrayal instead. According to Abby's First Law, I was expected to get a lot of love from Myra, so much love that it would compensate for the lack of love in my pre-Myra life, and that was exactly what was happening.

Going by what people around me observed, I had started looking much better than before and had also started talking a lot to people other than Myra. The credit for it went to Myra. Before we started staying together, I could keep my thoughts and tensions buried in my heart without anyone knowing anything about it. But now, whenever she noticed that I was in a pensive mood, she sat with me and forced me to convert the thoughts in my mind into words in my mouth. She did this every single time and eventually turned me into someone who became restless if he did not speak up whenever any thought crossed his mind. This change enabled her to understand me inside out, so much so that she could almost always read my mind.

A tremendous level of understanding developed between us and we could communicate without words, through our mutual understanding. To be honest, she was better at understanding me than I was at understanding her, or even myself.

But there was a flipside to my turning so vocal and uninhibited. Whenever I got angry, I spoke unrestrained and hurt people with my words, as opposed to my previous self who kept his mouth compulsorily shut when he was angry because he knew one said hurtful things when angry. I thought of it as a negative quality, but Myra always counted it as positive.

"One should speak up when he is angry or tensed to get rid of the anger or tension. If he suppresses these emotions, it can lead to problems like high blood pressure and depression," Myra used to tell me.

This quality undoubtedly brought Myra and me closer to each other, but it was also the one that distanced us from our close relatives over a period of time. Not everyone appreciated a person who called a spade a spade. They got offended or hurt when we spoke the bitter truth, and discounted the fact that we were very clean at heart and could be trusted blindly.

Talking about friends, or acquaintances to be precise, the people who had flocked to me during my ISB and OW days vanished just like the inner Abby had told me. I was still a struggling entrepreneur to them and nobody wanted to keep in touch with a struggler. Many of my ISB mates thought that I would not be of any use to them in their foreseeable future and distanced themselves from me. Regular phone calls from a couple of close IIT friends also stopped. I tried to keep in touch with them by always being the first one to call, but it was hurting my self-respect a lot. So, I stopped calling them and never received calls from them either. All of this reinforced my belief in the fact that friendship in today's world is need-based and not emotion-based. You don't necessarily have to be an extrovert to have many friends; you need to be successful and rich.

On the professional front, I managed Eduwiser from Mumbai, where I set up our corporate office. In 2011, Eduwiser was listed among India's top five educational publishing companies in a report prepared by a global management consultancy firm. For a startup that was just two years old, it was a big achievement.

In the job market, it seemed as if I was still in demand. Mouth-watering offers kept coming my way, trying their best to distract and derail me, but I kept rejecting them in the pursuit of my dreams.

I had a perfect life in every sense of the word. I had a perfect wife and a perfect career. After all, how many of us get to wake up every morning to the woman of our dreams? How many of us have wives who really love us? How many of us love our job and are satisfied with it? How many of us make a living out of something we love doing? These are things that elude most of the people and I was lucky to not be one among them.

13

November 2011 – August 2012
Mumbai

Both Myra and I were of the view that together, we were invincible. Whether or not we actually were, is a different thing. We used to wonder how talented a man or a woman would be if he or she had the qualities of both of us. Since we had never come across such a talented human until late 2011, we thought it was time to create one. God was kind and the arrow hit the bull's eye in the first unprotected attempt itself.

Since the pregnancy strip test was giving inconclusive results, we decided to take the confirmatory blood test. I went alone to collect the report on 1 January. The plan was to see the test result with Myra after I reached home, but curiosity got the better of me and made me open the test report envelope before that. With a fluttering heart, I unfolded the report only to get the best New Year's gift ever; the result was positive. Myra was pregnant! I went blank. My lips moved as if to say something that I could neither hear nor comprehend. Tears of happiness blessed my eyes, blurring my vision. I wiped my tears and raced my car back home to give Myra the good news.

Myra was equally excited and started jumping cautiously when I told her of the result. She hugged me tight with a smiling face that was crying too.

Everyone was happy on hearing the good news which we conveyed after the sixth week sonography. But all of them were busy in their own world. Nobody had the time to come to Mumbai and take care of Myra or support us during our pregnancy. Throughout my life until then, I had observed that mothers usually took care of their pregnant daughters, be it at the mother's home or at the daughter's. But our case was an exception. Not one to depend on others, I took it upon myself to take care of my Myra and my baby.

I changed my daily schedule a little. While I was available for calls from office during the day, most of my office work happened during the night, after putting Myra to sleep by singing songs to her.

My day time job responsibilities included cooking Myra's favourite food (she did not like what the cook made) and serving them to her on the bed, massaging her legs, putting the anti-stretch mark cream on her belly, helping her with her daily exercises to ensure a normal delivery, giving her all the medications on time, etc. To pamper her even more, I gave her a pedicure once a week. She was not allowed to go for her medical tests or doctor visits in an auto-rickshaw or a cab or with any other driver but me. Just like we feed milk to a newborn every three hours throughout the night, I gave her small quantities of

Bournvita in cold milk every couple of hours during the nights to keep her acidity problems at bay.

"I am so lucky to have you Abby. I don't think anyone in this world, including Mummy, would have taken care of me the way you are," Myra told me once.

"That's because you are my princess and I want you to live like one," I told her.

"Abby, I am turning uglier each day. I have put on so much weight and have started having pimples on my face too. I have no idea how ugly I would become by the time our baby is born. Will you still love me as much as you do now?" she asked.

"You will always look beautiful to me, Jaan, because your soul is beautiful. And about your outward appearance, however you look, I would consider that as perfect. If you turn skinny, I would consider skinny as perfect, and if you turn chubby, I would consider chubby as perfect," I replied.

The pregnancy was a blessing for our relationship because it helped our love reach a new high. We were so much into each other that we were not afraid of dying, but were terrified of dying separately at different points in time.

Weeks melted into months and we reached the final month of our pregnancy. People around started telling us various tricks to find out the sex of our baby. For example, there was a ring technique, the water-drop technique, the shape of the baby bump, etc. Somehow, Myra and I had a gut feeling that we would be blessed with a baby boy who we had decided to name as Rey.

Everyone who had had kids warned us that our lives would change completely after the baby's arrival. So, we started planning for the changes we expected the baby to bring in our lives, based on what we had seen around with other new parents. We were confident that we would be the best parents to the best kid in the world.

Mom flew down to Mumbai to be with us on the big day that soon arrived. I was there with Myra in the labour room during the delivery, holding her hand tightly and asking her to continue with her Lamaze breathing technique while Myra kept churning out the choicest of expletives, and that too in Hindi, for one of the nurses who had been a little cruel to her in bursting her water-bag. The anger gave her the much-needed strength and distracted her from the pain she was going through. After about half an hour of struggle, my cub was finally born.

"Congratulations Jaan! Rey has arrived and he looks exactly like you," I caressed Myra's forehead and whispered in her ear to let her know that we were blessed with a son.

"Rey…," Myra sighed and dozed off, tiredness and the effect of anesthesia overpowering her.

Mom had already been informed about Rey's arrival. When I came out of the labour room, she hugged me tightly and said with tears in her eyes, "Congratulations, beta! I can't believe you are a father now. I am so happy for Myra and you."

"Thanks Mom. It is all because of your blessings," I replied.

I took Mom's leave and went out of the nursing home to celebrate with a cigarette that I had not touched for the last nine months. Totally unaware that the most challenging part of my life was waiting to engulf me, I winked at god, looking up in the sky, "Thank you god, for being there. Thank you for Rey. I love you!"

God must have smiled back saying, "Your life of tests is over. The tests of your life will now begin. Be ready for it."

14

September 2012 – December 2014
Mumbai

"Just like a business goes through a cycle with alternating ups and downs, our life also goes through a cycle with alternating ups and downs."

This was my Second Law of Life. As fate would have it, the law validated itself again in my life.

Contrary to our expectations, Rey's arrival threw such a big curve to the vehicle of our lives that it overturned, flushing all our initial planning down the drain. Rey was a very difficult kid to handle, so difficult that no one we knew had seen a more difficult kid than him.

A couple of weeks after Rey's birth, Mom left for Patna to be with Dad. Her departure from Mumbai marked the arrival of a huge workload in my personal life. Since Myra was still recovering and was not in a position to share the responsibilities at home, I had to take care of Rey, Myra and our home.

Myra was an anxious and a paranoid mother who wanted Rey to sleep for at least eighteen hours a day. But Rey was a light sleeper. Added to that, it took a good forty-five minutes to put him to sleep every single time he woke up, and that too, by walking around cradling him and singing lullabies to him. Obviously, Myra's impractical and impossible objective was rarely achieved. Since she was not physically strong enough to hold Rey in her arms and walk around, it was my responsibility to put him to sleep whenever he got up, be it during the day or during the night. During the day, it was still fine, but at nights, it was a challenge to maintain my sanity. To let Myra sleep peacefully at night, I often used to take Rey to the living room to put him to sleep and took rest via a series of power naps of ten to fifteen minutes each while sitting on the couch with Rey sleeping on my lap.

For the first two months, Myra breastfed Rey. But after that, he refused it, and the responsibility of feeding him formula milk with bottles also fell into my lap. Myra wanted him to be fed every two hours, even during the nights, and I had to ensure he got his milk on time. Rey was not the kind of kid who would effortlessly drink the milk he was given. Throughout his feeding time, I used to keep praying to god, "Please god, make him have sufficient milk. Please, please, please… and don't make him puke."

More often than not, he did not have the entire milk. In such cases, I was expected to stick to Myra's demand of feeding him the remaining milk somehow – like, by walking around the room, holding him with one hand and feeding him with the other, or singing lullabies in a scary voice, etc.

Myra's fingers were allergic to detergents and soaps due to which the responsibility of washing and sterilizing milk bottles also got added to my new job description. For the same 'allergy' reason, changing Rey's diapers every time he soiled them was also my duty, because Myra would have to wash her hands with soap after changing the diaper. Though I bought gloves for her so that she could at least wash the bottles and relieve me of some workload, she refused to take up this responsibility saying, "Infants get severe stomach infection from milk bottles if they are not washed properly. You wash the bottles very nicely, so you do it because we can't take a risk with Rey's health."

Rey had the problem of reflux, due to which he used to puke even the last molecule of anything he had in his tummy, during or right after the feed. And this happened about four to five times a day, on an average. Since Myra insisted that he be fed again immediately after he puked, I had to go through the painful, tiring cycle of feeding him again.

Since a newborn's body parts are very fragile, we massaged Rey ourselves. Between Myra and I, Myra thought I massaged Rey better, with the proper pressure. So, I had to become his masseur and massage him twice every day.

There wasn't much support from family since nobody could come and stay with us for more than a week because of their other commitments. For a week that they did visit, they could not handle Rey. Anyone who tried putting Rey to sleep or tried to feed him failed miserably at it.

We did think about keeping a maid. But the thought of leaving Rey with the maid for even five minutes made us feel guilty about being bad parents, and so, we postponed the plan. We were also apprehensive of letting any maid handle Rey because we could not trust anyone with our baby. With his cries and tantrums,

Rey used to exhaust our brains to an extent that they would stop working. Since we were Rey's parents, we could not get angry at him beyond a point. But a maid probably could. Imagine what she could do! She could hurt him in our absence and we would have only been able to repent our decision after that.

I would be wrong if I said that I did all the work related to Rey and Myra did nothing. Of course, she did help me. It was a split of 80-20; I did 80% of the work, while she did the balance 20%. I knew she was physically weaker than me and could not perform certain tasks such as putting Rey to sleep, etc., but what irked me the most was that she did not even try to help me in things where she easily could have. Whatever I did for Rey to see off the first few months for Myra to recover, was made my permanent duty. She also deliberately did not let me go to office, due to which I got very little time to work for Eduwiser.

Things did not change much over the next few months. However, there was a silver lining to my dark clouds. Rey grew very close to me. Normally, kids look out for their Mom, but Rey looked out for me, much to the disappointment of Myra. The first word that Rey spoke was 'Da' instead of 'Ma' or 'Mumma'. This word was his simpler version of 'Daddy'. As soon as I would vanish from his sight, he would start crawling around the entire house looking for me with his cute shouts of "Da, Da, Daaaa…". This annoyed Myra. Though she used to tell people around that Rey's 'Da' meant 'Ma', but both of us knew the truth.

When Rey started eating, he mostly wanted me to feed him. When he slept, I either had to lie beside him or had to place beside him a pillow with my t-shirt on it, with my smell, to make him think I was sleeping next to him. Whenever he got hurt or cried, his hands reached out for me instead of Myra, causing her a lot of embarrassment. When such things started happening in public, Myra started getting very irritated with both, Rey and me. Relatives often remarked, "Abby is Rey's Mom." While it was an honour for me, it was a disgrace for Myra who failed to understand that whatever was happening with her was nothing but a perfect example of 'you reap what you sow'.

"You did all the chores for Rey just to snatch him from me, right? This was your strategy," she said one day.

"Jaan, you asked me to do everything and I did them to help you," I replied.

"Don't act so innocent, because you are not! You are one great actor," she said.

"Actor? I am telling you the truth. I did things to help you and because I love Rey. I did not do so much to hear all this crap from you, Myra," I retorted.

"Shut up! Now I can see your true colors, Abby."

"Fine, if you think I did everything as a part of some covert plan, you take care of Rey from now on. I have no problem with that."

Letting Myra handle Rey did not help, as he needed my touch in everything. As a result, she shoved all his responsibilities down my throat again. I was going crazy taking care of Rey and Myra, while being exposed to Myra's acerbic remarks on my so-called strategy to alienate her from Rey.

"Why are you doing this to me, god? You know what is happening, you are seeing all of it, aren't you? Please do something," I kept telling god, but my prayers fell on deaf ears.

I failed to understand his intentions of putting our lives through such a test. He knew Myra and I were very strong together. Maybe, he wanted to see us fight against each other to check who was stronger. I got so pissed with him one day that I collected all the idols from every corner of our house and locked them in the puja room saying, "There is no god for me now. I am done with him." When sanity prevailed, I did apologize for my behaviour and it probably cooled him down. Well, that is what I thought at that time. He made me pay a huge price for it a few years later.

Come to think of it, surviving that period of my life was nothing short of a miracle. Things turned marginally better when Rey turned a year-and-a-half old. But it was too late and the damage was already done. In addition to my already existing problem of cervical spondylitis, I was gifted with lower back and knee pains. I was always known for my strong memory, but I became so forgetful that I used to forget what I went to a particular room for. This was because while Myra and Rey were taken care of, I was left ignored. I never got time to think about myself and there was no one in this world, including Myra, who cared about my health. The fact that Myra did not care for me anymore showed in her actions and words. Even if I had fever or migraine or spondylitis pain, she behaved as if nothing had happened and still expected me to do the household stuff like earlier. So, I stopped caring for her too.

While things kept getting better each day with respect to Rey, Myra and I continued to drift apart. The fact that both of us had different parenting styles made things worse. She was a 'Hitler Mom' who wanted Rey to do everything according to her rules, some of which were logical, while many of them were not. On the contrary, I was a 'Cool Dad' who did not want to tie Rey down with rules. I wanted to give him some breathing space to explore things around and satisfy his curiosity, which often led to him dirtying the house a little. Myra was finicky about cleanliness and would get mad at me for letting Rey dirty the house. I didn't agree to her 'iron-hand' style of parenting and she didn't agree to my 'breathing space' style of parenting. I thought she was being sacrosanct about her parenting rules and I often got irritated with her because she was not open to any feedback or discussion. She thought she was always right. According to her, whatever I did, however I did it, was wrong. The girl who had loved everything about me at one point of my life started criticizing me for every single thing – the way I looked, the way I walked, the way I talked, the way I ate, the way I drove our car, etc. She became perennially rude to me and treated me as if I was actually her slave.

Finally, my patience failed the stress test it was subjected to by Myra, and I gave in to my anger. When good fails to win over evil, the good needs to turn evil and fight back. I had had enough of Myra and decided to behave evil like her to make her go through what she made me experience every single day.

My decision to fight back the domestic abuse she was inflicting upon me backfired. It led to extreme emotional outbursts from her; something as extreme as hitting me one night while I was putting Rey to sleep on my lap, and saying, "I will murder you, fucker."

I cursed myself for loving and marrying such a girl. I seriously could not believe I had sacrificed so much for a girl like her. She was not the Myra I loved. I always told her that I loved her because her soul was beautiful and that her physical appearance did not matter. Now, her soul had turned ugly. My love and respect for Myra reduced. On multiple occasions, I felt like killing myself, but did not go ahead because of Rey. I knew he would be left alone in this cruel world if I was gone. I also thought about divorcing Myra, but hung on to the marriage for Rey, as I did not want him to suffer. The only solution left to me was to give our marriage another shot.

I tried my best to obey most of her orders to make our marriage work and whenever I did so, she was very loving; but as soon as I expressed my disagreement with her on anything, she got violent and abusive. And whenever she turned abusive, I just could not keep my mouth shut. Since both Myra and I were strong-headed individuals, clashes were inevitable, but an argument on anything as simple as how to put a pen in a pen-stand is something which is a writing on the wall for any relationship. I knew it was only a matter of a few months or years before we would go our separate ways. Only a miracle could save our marriage.

By the time Rey was two years old, he started sleeping throughout the night. We also enrolled him at a play school. So, I finally started getting time to focus on my other baby, Eduwiser, which I had been forced to ignore all this while, and which needed me badly if it were to remain in business. I became a lot calmer than I had been in the last two years. I set aside my ego and took the initiative to apologize to Myra.

"Myra, I am sorry for whatever happened from my side. If I hurt you in any way, I sincerely apologize," I told Myra one night.

"Finally, you realized your mistake and apologized. Why do you have so much ego, Abby? When you already knew you were wrong, why didn't you apologize to me earlier? Things would have improved long ago," she replied accusing me, as if I was the only one who had committed mistakes in the last two years.

"I said sorry for hurting you. That doesn't mean whatever I did in these two years was wrong."

"Then there is no point apologizing. You just cannot admit your mistakes."

"Let us not get started again. I do not want to talk about what happened, why it happened, who was wrong and who was right. I want to start afresh for our future."

"See, this is your problem. You are not ready to discuss. Why should we talk about what you want to, when you are not ready to talk about what I want to?"

"Ok baba, I am sorry. I made all the mistakes. Is it fine now?" I said eating up my ego to put an end to our bickering.

"Do you know the meaning of saying sorry? It means that you will not repeat your mistakes."

"I will try not to. Now tell me, what do you expect from me?"

"I want you to get a job."

"A job? Where did this come from?"

"Yes, a job in a reputed company, and if possible, out of India, because I want to settle abroad."

"Settling abroad is fine, but why do I need to get a job for that? We can settle abroad even if I continue working for Eduwiser."

"I do not want you to continue with Eduwiser."

"But why? You want a lot of money and you want to settle abroad; Eduwiser can give us both."

"It can never succeed."

"Please do not say anything negative about my firm."

"What I said is a fact. I don't like Eduwiser at all."

"You don't like Eduwiser? Can you please elaborate on that?"

"I feel embarrassed in front of people when I tell them that my husband runs a publishing company. It is a low-class business. I will feel proud of you when you work for some multinational company."

"But isn't Eduwiser something that you boast of when you get into an altercation with any outsider? Eduwiser is my baby. I have worked day and night to bring it to the level it is at. How can you ask me to leave it? Do you even know that it is considered to be one of the top brands in education? Don't you think that setting up such a company with distributors across the country is a big achievement? Why are you ashamed of it?"

"Call it my archaic mindset or whatever, but I want you to be in a job. I still think you cannot run Eduwiser because Kayasthas cannot be successful in business. They are meant to work in a job."

"I have heard this horrendous reasoning before. So you were the source of questions that your parents had asked me when I had returned from Dubai to start Eduwiser. Good job, Myra! See, the thing is that your mindset is your problem, not mine. I run my firm with my capabilities, not with my caste. Eduwiser is my baby and I will never leave it. I have dreams that I have to turn into reality. Working for someone else does not fit into my grand scheme of things."

"Don't you realize that you will be spoiling two more lives along with yours? I had always dreamt of my husband having a high-paying job and settling abroad. When you joined OW in Dubai, I thought my dreams came true, but then you shattered them. You don't value my dreams, you never have. You don't care about what I want. You are so selfish Abby, you are only thinking about yourself."

"Aren't you selfish too? Are you thinking about my dreams? No! Then, how do you expect me to think about yours? And by the way, how can your dreams or goals in life be about *my* professional life? You should probably have dreams related to your professional life Myra, not mine."

"Fine, then join a job and handle Eduwiser with it."

"Whatever one does, he should give his full share of mind to it. If I work in a job and handle Eduwiser part-time, I will screw up both, my job and Eduwiser. So joining a job is not a feasible option."

"Nobody can win an argument against you. You have to argue every single time. Why can't you stop thinking and just do what I tell you to?"

"I can't take an impractical decision just because the person I love is asking me to. Listen Myra, your dream is to settle abroad and I will make sure it comes true. Whether it is through Eduwiser or some XYZ company, it should not matter to you," I said bringing an end to the discussion that was initiated to repair our weakened ties.

When Rey was more or less settled, the squabbles over parenting styles gave way to arguments on the job issue. Myra nagged me almost daily about quitting Eduwiser and joining a job. I guess that was the time when I started drifting even further away from her. She was thinking only about herself and did not have any respect for me, my work and my dream.

An entrepreneur's life is very lonely. He is a very positive and confident person, but even such a person starts doubting himself at times. Many a times, he cries, but nobody gets to know. The people around only see his success or failure, not the moments of doubt and crisis he goes through. Only he is a witness to his umpteen small successes and failures throughout his journey. There is a special quality in all successful entrepreneurs – they motivate themselves and fight back. These people are very serious about keeping away from negative people who discourage and demotivate them, who keep telling them, "You can't do it!"

With me, the case was similar, except that I did not have the option of running away from the person who was apparently the most negative, demotivating and discouraging of all – Myra. Whatever project I undertook and informed her about, her first remark used to be, "Eduwiser cannot be successful, no matter what you do. Sell it off and join a job," instead of motivating and supporting me.

Committed to making our relationship work, Myra and I kick-started our old tradition of partying in my study at night. Nine out of ten times, the session ended in an avoidable heated argument on who was more selfish, Myra or I. I think we both were.

The sales experience at Eduwiser had made me very persistent in my efforts to convince people. So, when Myra started her round of nagging during one of our gossip sessions at night, I introduced her to Abby's Third Law of Life:

"Each of us in this world has been gifted with at least one talent that he can use to get rich and famous."

"Discovering that talent is the biggest hurdle in getting him the life of his dreams. Most people go to their graves totally ignorant about the talent they were gifted with. Myra, I have already overcome the challenge of discovering my talent and finding my calling. It is to be an entrepreneur in the educational sector. Do not force me to join a job because I will not be happy in it. And if I am not happy doing what I am doing, how will I be able to keep Rey and you happy? I need your support Myra," I tried to convince her.

"Ok Abby, do what you want to, but I will not support you in it. That is final. The maximum I can do is that I will not be after your life to join a job and I will never say that Eduwiser will fail," Myra said.

What Myra said was enough for me. At least she would not demotivate me now. But her promise was just casual talk and she started pestering me again within a week's time.

"Myra, I have been able to help you with Rey until now only because I had my own company and so, could manage my work hours. Had I been in a job, my employer would have fired me right away," I made another try to bring her around to my point of view.

"Had you been working in a job, I would have handled Rey alone because I would have had no other option. Join a job and get freedom from taking care of Rey," she offered.

"Why don't you take care of Rey right now to give me more time to work for Eduwiser? That would be very helpful."

"No, I will not do it for Eduwiser. I will support you only if you join a job. If you can't let go of Eduwiser, divide your time between your job and Eduwiser. Handle Eduwiser after office hours and during the weekends."

"Apart from the 'share of mind' argument I gave you a few days ago, I will also not get time for Rey and you in that case. For me, my family time is very important."

"I am fine with it. In any case, there is no love left between us. If you join a job, at least I will feel proud and we will have a regular income. That would mean real happiness."

"Really? And do you think I will be able to survive with such a schedule? What if something happens to me?"

"You already are as useless as a dead person for me. It would not affect me."

Her reply stung my heart and rendered me speechless. I took her leave to go to the washroom because it was getting difficult for me to hold back my tears. Myra had a sharp tongue, so sharp she could cut a diamond with it. She probably did not realize the amount of pain she induced in me through her comments and unfiltered thoughts.

"You deserve to suffer, Myra. God is watching and he will punish you one day," I said looking at the helpless Abby in the washroom mirror.

In a matter of a few days, she again had her emotional outburst when I tried to protect Rey from her merciless spanking because he was scared to sleep alone in the dimly-lit bedroom.

"You are a worthless, good-for-nothing guy, who could never become a good husband, a good father, a good son, a good brother, or a good friend. That is the reason Shalini left you. And that is the reason you have no friend. Die and go to hell, nobody needs you," she said.

"I did not tell you about Shalini dumping me for you to make fun of me. And I don't need you to tell me what I could or could not be for other people. Your soul has become so ugly, Myra. Trust me, you will die a painful lonely death and even hell will not accept you," I cursed her for hurting me over and over again with her words.

Arguments on trivial issues still happened on a regular basis, after which we would stop talking to each other for a few days. In fact, they happened every time we talked to each other. Myra had a number of friends she partied with on weekends or even weekdays. So, she could pour her heart out to them. She even used to call her sisters and Mummy to bitch about me. I, on the other hand, had no friends who I could talk to and vent out my feelings. I could not talk to my brothers or Mom-Dad about it, because it would have turned them against Myra, and I did not want that. I could not talk to Mummy and Hitler Dad because they would obviously support their daughter. All other relatives would have listened to me, but only with the intention of getting their hands on some spicy gossip about our marriage. I was therefore left sulking alone, talking to myself in the washroom mirror. Actually not alone, cigarettes were there to give me company. At twenty cigarettes a day, I became a chain smoker. I could only wish god gave me a true friend I could talk to and feel lighter. I had no idea a familiar hand was waiting to pull me out of the quagmire of crisis I was stuck in.

15

January 2015
Mumbai

Weeks rolled into months and landed us in January 2015. On the night of 23 January, I was busy wrapping up work on my Physics textbook. By the time I was done with it, it was already 7 a.m. of 24 January – my birthday. I was about to go to sleep for a couple of hours (before Rey woke up) when a birthday message on my Facebook messenger nudged the sleepiness out of me.

"Happy birthday Abby! May all your wishes come true. Have a great year ahead!" Shalini messaged.

"What a pleasant surprise so early in the morning! Thanks so much Shalini. How have you been?" I messaged back.

"I am good. How have you been?" she asked.

"I am fine, sleep-starved as always. Rey and work keep me very, very busy," I messaged.

"I know you are always awake. You are online whatever time of the day or night I check Facebook."

"You keep a tab on me?"

"Ummm… not deliberately, but subconsciously, I guess."

"Now that can mean a lot of things. Choose your words wisely, ma'am."

"I am not sure if I chose my words wisely, but I definitely chose them truthfully."

"Does that mean I still occupy some place in your heart?"

"You always have. You are my most beautiful past."

"Your most beautiful past?"

"Yes."

"If it was so beautiful, why did you turn it ugly by dumping me, Shalini?"

"Don't use that word 'dump'. It makes me feel very guilty."

"You know, I have been waiting to ask you my questions for the past eleven years. Why did you leave without even giving our love a chance? I loved you so much. You just broke up suddenly, despite me having told you that I would talk to your parents about our marriage. Why? Did you not love me enough to fight for me? Did you lie to me about your roka to get rid of me?"

"I have always loved you a lot, Abby. I have never felt as comfortable with anyone as I was with you; it was just that I kept myself constrained that time to prevent hurting my parents for my selfish reasons. I had asked Mom if she would consider a guy I loved, but belonged to a different caste. Without mincing her words, she told me that she would commit suicide if I ever even thought of such a thing. She told me that our whole extended family would shun us if they got to know about it as it would set a bad example for my younger sister and cousins. She got upset with me saying that she had not sent me so far to do these things. I was so scared of the consequences that I did not bring up this topic with her or Dad again. I did not lie to you about my roka. I got engaged to my current husband in 2004, the same year we broke up."

"You did not even care to call me once after that. The least you could do was apologize to me, but you never did. My love for you deserved at least that much respect. Instead, you were rude. Didn't your conscience pinch you?"

"I am really very sorry for what I did. If it was possible to go back in time and correct my mistake, believe me, I would give my life for it. But I know nothing can happen now."

"Tell me the truth Shalini, were you seeing anyone else that time? I have a gut feeling that you were."

"Ok, I have a confession to make. Please do not take me otherwise. After we broke up in April that year, I had another short-lived relationship with one of my batchmates, Sunny."

"See, I told you. My gut feelings are usually correct! Please go on, I want to know everything that happened."

"He was a friend since our first year and we got a little close during our internship together right after our break up, as we spent a lot of time together. I got forcefully engaged to my current husband, Prashant in October. But by December, I was sure I wanted to marry Sunny and not Prashant. I talked to my parents about it, but they refused, leading to a lot of arguments. I even asked our close relatives to support me which they did, but my parents did not budge."

"This implies you loved Sunny more than you loved me, because you chose to fight for him, but you did not do the same in my case."

"I fought with my parents for him because by that time, I had developed some courage."

"True love empowers one with courage to fight for it. If you did not have the courage to fight for your love for me, it wasn't true love in the first place."

"I have never loved anyone more than I have loved you, Abby. I admit there was a connection with Sunny, but it wasn't as strong as it was with you."

"Then what happened?"

"When I tried to get in touch with Sunny to ask him to send his parents to talk to mine for our marriage, he just took off on me and I got married to Prashant a year later."

"Took off on you? You mean, he just vanished? How can he vanish all of a sudden? He must have said something."

"No, he did not say anything; he disappeared. He ignored all the calls I made to him and never called back or got in touch. Maybe, the feelings were one-sided."

"One last question. You started seeing Sunny in May-June. How could you get into a relationship with him when your situation at home had not changed and you still did not have the courage to fight for your love that time? If you could not hurt your parents for me, how could you take another relationship forward knowing that it would also make you hurt them? And if you had to get into a relationship with someone, it had to be me again. You should have got back in touch with me. Why did you get involved with a new guy?"

"I was ashamed of myself for treating you the way I had. So, I could not gather the strength to call you. Maybe the geographical distance between us also had some part to play."

"All that does not matter if the love is genuine and strong. When love is weak, there are cracks in the relationship through which such excuses leak. He must be better-looking than me, isn't it? I mean, I was more intelligent than him, at least on paper. There was no match for my nature and loyalty. So, it had to be my looks that disappointed you."

"I will send you his Facebook profile link, you take a call on whether he was better-looking or worse."

"I am a very self-aware man, Shalini. I know I did not look great that time. I also know that I was one of those undesirable soft guys, who would always be polite and agreeable. Besides that, you did not even know me that well because we just met once during our relationship of three years. Had I been in your place, I, too, would have rejected a guy like me. So, you did the right thing. I have no complaints from you. In fact, I want to thank you for answering all of my unanswered questions that had been haunting me for more than a decade. I had thought I would have to take all my questions to the grave with me. Thank you for giving me this windfall of answers."

"You must be very angry with me right now, isn't it? I am sorry Abby."

"For the last eleven years, I have been very, very angry with you; so angry that you can't even imagine its intensity. After all, you had insulted my love. But right now, I am not. I feel at peace with myself. Thank you again for this wonderful birthday gift. I do admit I feel like a fool right now and am feeling terribly bad for that innocent, poor me who loved you more than anything else in this world."

"Whatever happened has happened Abby. If I can do anything to make up for all the pain I have subjected your heart to, you name it and I will do it."

"I can't punish you or avenge myself on you. How can I do that to someone I considered my world at one point of time? However, you can do one thing to make up for your mistake. Be my true friend forever and never betray me like you did earlier."

"That is a reward for me Abby, not a punishment."

"You got your payback when Sunny betrayed you. Everyone commits mistakes, but very few own them up and you are one of them. You had the option of hiding the truth from me, but you didn't. You have changed, and I think you deserve a second chance from me, though as a good friend. I hope I can trust you this time," I said because I did not want to let go of an opportunity to have a trustworthy friend I had always needed.

"I will not disappoint you. I will be there with you as a friend whenever you need me," she said.

We then bid goodbye to each other after exchanging our numbers. I was not surprised by what she told me, but it still shook me from inside. The feeling took some time to sink in. My heart ached for that unconditionally loving and naïve Abby who lost a part of his heart when Shalini left him for another guy.

I was lost in my thoughts, only to be interrupted by Myra's loud voice.

"Happy birthday Abby! Hope you have a healthy, wealthy and happy life, with me," she said.

"Thanks Myra," I said.

"You are up so early?" she asked.

"I never slept. I was working on my next book and have just sent it to the press for printing," I replied.

"You and your work. Let's not get into that today. What are your plans?"

"You tell me."

"Since it is your birthday, you tell me how you want to spend it."

"I need to recalibrate my brain and heart for a couple of hours. Can you take Rey to some play area? I want to be with myself for some time. After that, we can probably go to a mall and then to a restaurant," I requested Myra.

"Sure, no problem. You take your time. I will feed him and take him to the play area. You can relax," she replied.

I went to my study to talk to the inner Abby and settle my ruffled mind.

"I am blank. Do you have anything to tell me?" I asked the inner Abby.

"Of course I do. Remember, I am your heart and I know things that you don't. Now listen. There was one girl Shalini, whom you loved so much, but who did not care to fight for you and your relationship. Instead, she left you for someone else. When you guys were together, she never showed any respect for your love and even then you never got angry with her. You always tried to understand her and apologized to her, even when she was at fault. Today also, you forgave her for whatever she did. And there is this girl Myra, who left everything for you, who always kept you as priority, who fought with the closest of her friends and relatives for you and who never left you for anyone, not even her parents. But you hold a grudge against her and fight with her on every issue. You were never like this. You were always loving, caring and understanding, but you turned into a monster when life threw a challenge to your relationship," said the inner Abby.

"Go on, I am listening," I said.

"You always say that you are an epitome of justice and fairness, but I believe you have been unfair to Myra. You have always kept that innocent, loving and understanding Abby hidden under the aegis of a fake, arrogant and egoist one. Myra deserves the original version of you, who was all heart in matters of love and who invested all his emotions into his relationship without the fear of being hurt. Abby, it is ok to be emotionally weak in love. That is what love is all about. Please bring your original self back and let Myra enjoy that privilege because she deserves it. She loves you so much!" the inner Abby continued.

"But even she has become a monster since the time Rey was born. She does not care about me at all and does not support me in my work. She says it would not even matter to her if I died," I argued.

"You are not a stranger to something called postpartum depression. Before her pregnancy, she was one of the hottest girls around. She looked beautiful in whatever she wore. People used to stare at her with appreciation. During her pregnancy and after it, she lost all her physical attractiveness. While her outward appearance does not matter to you, it does to her. She was and still is so conscious of the way she looks. Imagine the kind of mental trauma she has been battling since her pregnancy days. She is in depression, Abby. You cannot expect sanity from somebody going through depression, which is a serious illness. Many women commit suicide due to their postpartum depression. You should thank god she is still fighting it, though without you. She is ill and needs your help, not your anger. She needs love and attention, and above all, she needs to feel good about herself. She has many friends, but you know they don't care about what she is going through internally.

"Regarding not supporting you in your work, she does not let you go to office or anywhere else because she wants you to be with her at all times. She gets restless when she does not see you around. You mistook these signals as her way to torture you. Chew on it for a little while and you will realize, these are signs of extreme love which blesses only a few souls in this materialistic world. And here you are, the luckiest unlucky soul who wants to let go of his love, Myra," the inner Abby hit the nail on the head.

"I cannot agree more with you. I am feeling so ashamed of my behaviour that has been nothing short of being childish. I was the one who used to keep preaching to newlyweds that if you want a marital relationship to work, one of the persons should be calm and quiet when the other gets angry; if both get angry at the same time, the relationship will fail. And see what I was doing, getting angry at the same time as Myra. My primary aim in life was to keep Myra happy. I did not even realize when my secondary aim of entrepreneurship became the primary one. From now on, Myra will be my priority and everything I do, will be for her. Please tell me, where do I start from? Things have really spun out of control," I said.

"Nothing is out of control because I know she still loves you. You don't have to make a checklist of things you should do.

Just be yourself, the original Abby, not the fake one, and things will find their way back. The fake one is good for your business, though," the inner Abby said.

This time, the mind and the heart were on the same page. Without any delay, I left for the play area to present Myra with the Abby she deserved.

16

January 2015 – October 2015
Mumbai

The first thing I did when I reached the play area was hug Myra and apologize for everything hurtful I had done. I promised her that I would do whatever it takes to make our marriage work and ensure her happiness.

Touched by my gesture, Myra hugged me tightly and said with tears in her eyes, "I have never felt as lonely as I have in the past two-and-a-half years, Abby. Though you were present physically, I was left to fend for myself. Don't you ever do that again. You know you mean the world to me, and I need you physically and emotionally."

"Never ever, Myra. I love you too. I will be the best husband in the world," I said kissing her on the lips without caring about the people around, who I noticed passed faint smiles to each other.

Love made a powerful comeback between Myra and me, making the garden of our relationship bloom again with flowers of love. And what a date for the comeback, my birthday! Since Myra's dream was to settle abroad, I decided to sell off my dream – Eduwiser, to realize hers and make an entry back into the rat race of the corporate world.

Getting acquired by a bigger fish in the pond was easy and quick. A global publishing company had been requesting me for the past one year to consider its proposal of acquiring Eduwiser. I said yes to its offer and exited Eduwiser fifty crores richer. Selling off my dream did hurt, but the pain was a price I was willing to pay for Myra's happiness. The deal happened in February, but I kept Myra in the dark about it because I wanted to buy her a penthouse in Dubai as her surprise birthday gift. She had her birthday on 11 October, and I wanted to gift her the penthouse along with the news that we were shifting to Dubai for good by early next year. Had I told her about the deal, the penthouse and the Dubai relocation news would have been obvious gifts, not surprise ones.

Myra and I painted the town red when the Eduwiser deal happened. I was celebrating my windfall while she was celebrating the second innings of our love (as she knew nothing about the deal). Keeping her unaware of Eduwiser's buyout was easy as she did not follow my professional life and never had any idea about my bank balance. Though Mom-Dad knew about the deal, I requested them to keep the deal a secret from Myra.

"Abby, I have never told you that you write really well. Why don't you write a book?" she said during one of our gossip sessions at home.

"I have already," I replied.

"I am talking about a fiction novel, not the educational textbooks that you have already written. I love your writing and going by the responses your articles get, I am sure people love it too. Why don't you write a novel based on our love story? I would love to be the heroine of your novel. Trust me, people will love it."

"I don't have the time. I love writing and I really wish I could find time for writing a novel."

"I will support you. How much time do you need to write it?"

"Two to three months if I work on it full-time."

"Done, I give you three months to write it. I will take care of Rey alone, you take care of my novel. I want it as my birthday gift this year."

"Your wish, my command but don't back off with your support."

"I promise I won't."

From the next day itself, I started working on my first novel with Myra as its female lead. Apart from writing the novel, the time that she gave me was used up in a couple of short trips to Dubai to search and finalize a penthouse for her. Whenever I made those trips, I kept her under the impression that I was going to some Tier 2 Indian city for Eduwiser's work.

By the time May ended, I had finished my novel and submitted my proposal to leading publishing houses. Though Myra begged me to let her read the novel, I told her she could read it when I gifted her the first published copy.

For the last couple of years, we had not celebrated 19 July – our court marriage anniversary. But this year, I planned a special surprise like old times. On the night of 18 July, Myra slept off before midnight (probably because she was not expecting any gift or surprise from me). I took a long LED light-strip and put its one end in our bedroom, right beside our bed on which she was sleeping, while its other end was made into a loop and put on the dining table in the living room. At the centre of the loop, I placed a sparkling diamond necklace. On her phone, I scheduled a reminder for midnight with the text, "Get up and follow the lights". Then I lay down beside her, waiting for the phone to ring and show her the reminder text. The trick worked and she followed the lights with an uncontrollable excitement on her face. Surprisingly, she was thrilled and touched more by my gesture than the diamond necklace I had bought for her.

"Thank you so much. I got my Abby back," she said with moist eyes.

"Now, it is my turn to surprise you," she continued and went to the washroom to bring a strip kind of thing.

"Two red lines on a pregnancy strip? Are we expecting again?" I said, my voice beaming with excitement.

"Well, the strip thinks so. I always asked you to use protection, but you never listened."

"You know I hate using it and I am glad I did not. Rey needed a lifelong friend."

"I did not want a baby right now, but after seeing your reaction, I am feeling happy too. Now, here is your second surprise."

"Black Ray Ban! Wow! I had wanted it for so long. Thank you so much Jaan," I said and hugged her for the wonderful return surprises she gave me.

When Myra woke up the next morning, I broke another exciting news to her, "A leading publishing company has agreed to publish my novel."

"See, I had told you! I knew you could do it," she said and jumped with joy.

"You deserve the credit for it. If it was not for you, I would have never written a novel," I responded.

A week later, I finally purchased a sprawling penthouse in Dubai Marina, a posh area in Dubai. I also booked our flight tickets to Dubai to ring in her birthday there.

I was expected to get the first copy of the novel in the first week of October, a perfect time, given that we had to leave for Dubai in the second week. Myra was getting restless as she could not wait to get her hands on my novel. I really had to try very hard to make her keep calm during our pregnancy, which was going as smooth as a knife through butter.

You know, things turn happy in the end only in novels and movies, to give people those happy endings that they love. But this was not some fairy tale going on in our lives. No one can escape Abby's Second Law of Life. Our relationship (and lives) had hit rock bottom, and then reached another all-time high. As expected, the law reared its head yet again, this time an ugly one to ruin our lives forever.

We were ten days away from Myra's birthday. I still had to inform her about our surprise Dubai trip so that we could do our packing. The penthouse surprise, however, had to wait until her birthday. I was supposed to get the first copy of my novel directly from the printing press (in Mumbai) the next evening, at around the same time when Myra had her routine sonography scheduled. I decided to postpone my plan of collecting the novel so that I could accompany her to the sonography clinic, but destiny had a plan of its own.

It was around 2 a.m. and Myra had already gone to sleep with Rey. I thought I would check my WhatsApp messenger one last time before retiring to bed. Finding Shalini online, I pinged her and started chatting with her casually. I told her about all the surprises I had planned for Myra's birthday and about my novel that was soon going to be out in the market. While chatting, I kept deleting the chat simultaneously so that Myra did not get to know about the surprises, just in case she checked my phone later.

Lady Luck scowled at me and Myra woke up. With the intention of scaring the shit out of me, she came running towards me, making a scary sound. Well, she did succeed in scaring me. She was so quick that I fumbled with my phone and could barely manage to lock it. In the process of locking it, the profile of the phone changed from silent to normal. As I kept my phone clutched in my hand, the messages from Shalini kept coming in, and with them came loud message beeps which sounded like death knells, "Ting, ting, ting...."

"Who are you chatting with so late at night? Show me," she said in a playful voice.

"No one," I said.

"Why are you getting nervous?" she asked reading my facial expression correctly.

"Nervous? I am not nervous," I replied.

"Show me the chat Abby. You were chatting with somebody whose name starts with 'S'," her playful voice gave way to a loud demanding one.

"I will not," I said bluntly as I had no idea how to beat around the bush and evade her scrutiny.

"You were talking to Shalini? Show me the chat right now!" she said in a voice that had started becoming weaker. I knew tears would follow next.

"Yes, I was. But I will not show the chat to you. It is my personal matter," I said.

"Your personal matter? Abby, hundreds of thoughts are coming to my mind right now. Please, I beg of you. Show me the chat."

"You don't trust me?"

"No, going by the way you are behaving, I do not. See, even if you were flirting with her or having a sex chat, I have no problem with that. But I need to see the chat."

"You should trust me like I do when you go out partying with guys alone."

"Abby, don't make me do something that both of us would regret later," she threatened me with her suicide, apparently.

"You know I am not scared of anyone's threats. If you are trying to threaten me with your suicide, go die! Where there is no trust, there is no love, however much we fake it."

"You can let me die because of Shalini, the girl who dumped you? Is she that important to you?"

"It is nothing of that sort Myra. See," I said and showed her the chat, most of which was already deleted. Just the last few messages were there in which Shalini had written that I was a good husband and that Myra was lucky to have me.

"This is not the complete chat. Why did you delete the earlier messages?" she asked with suspicion.

"Because I thought you would get hurt if you came to know that I was chatting with her. And I was neither flirting with her nor having a sex chat. She is not that kind of a girl. I was asking her why she dumped me and what happened after our break up."

"That is not something that would prompt you to delete the messages. I am missing something here. What is up between the two of you?"

"I was also bitching about you. It would have hurt you if you read it. Myra, relax! She is married and has a kid. The same is the case with me. Neither of us is interested in having an affair outside marriage. We are happy in our own lives," I said making my last attempt to hide the surprises I had planned for her.

"Why did you do this Abby? And that too when everything was going so well," she said with tears rolling down her cheeks.

"Listen Myra, I have done nothing wrong. Just trust me. Don't I trust you when you go out with guys at night? I can also accuse you of having a scene with one of them and doing all things forbidden. But I don't, because I trust you."

"Just get out of my sight and don't show me your face," she shouted at me.

Thinking she was pregnant and that her emotional outburst could lead to serious complications, I decided to keep mum. I had lost my cool a little in our argument and that was because she was questioning my loyalty in the relationship. But my love for her and our unborn baby made me control my temper.

The next morning, I noticed Shalini had been deleted and blocked on my WhatsApp, Facebook and phone. This irritated me to the hilt. I had always given Myra the trust and the freedom to befriend anyone she wanted to, and I expected the same in return. I added Shalini back, but she told me not to keep in touch with her as Myra had had a chat with her on Facebook the previous night. When she did not tell me the content of their conversation, I signed into Myra's Facebook account and read the chat in which Myra had sent her accusatory messages, to which Shalini had replied in a decent way, assuring Myra that there was nothing illicit going on between us.

I was so pissed with Myra, but I somehow controlled my urge to spit venom as I did not want a squabble at this stage of her pregnancy. So, I kept quiet and decided to give her a break from me by not showing my face to her that day. I changed my mind about going to the clinic with her in the evening for the sonography and decided to pick up my novel from the printing press instead. I asked the maid to go along with her and leave Rey at our neighbour, Arun's house. I left for the printing press in the afternoon after putting Rey to sleep, thinking that the copy of my novel along with my Dubai surprise plans (which I decided to unveil to her later that evening) would undoubtedly make her happy and things would get back to normal.

On my way to the press, I prayed when I crossed the famous Siddhivinayak Temple, "I will not fight with Myra again, Ganpati Bappa. Please make sure this is our last fight. I want nothing else."

One should always choose his words carefully while making a wish to god and leave no room for its misinterpretation. In my case, Bappa's little misinterpretation of my wish turned my life upside down, and inside out.

17

October 2015 – April 2016
Mumbai

I had to wait for more than two hours at the printing press to get my novel, but the wait was totally worth it. When I held the novel in my hands, it felt like I was holding Myra's dream, not the book. The cover looked outstanding; it had to, because Myra had designed it. I could not wait any longer to get back to Myra and show it to her. The mere thought of her excitement on seeing the novel as well as the Dubai e-tickets sent a tingling sensation through my body. I took out my phone to call Myra and let her know that I had her novel in my hand. She just had to wait for another hour and a half to get her hands on it.

When I unlocked my phone, I saw there were twenty-nine missed calls, twenty-four of them were from Arun, four were from some unknown numbers, but one call was from Myra. There were also multiple messages from Arun, like "Call back urgently", "Where the hell are you?", etc. I realized I had put my phone on silent while putting Rey to sleep in the afternoon and had forgotten to change the settings back to the normal ringtone mode.

Hundreds of thoughts, mostly negative, started fluttering in my mind. Rey was supposed to be at Arun's house at that time and had anything happened to Rey, the twenty-four missed calls would have been from Myra, not from Arun. Without any delay, I called up Myra to make sure she was fine. I kept praying for her well-being, while Myra's phone kept ringing. Finally, the call was received and I was relieved.

"Thank god, you are...," I said only to be interrupted by an unexpected male voice.

"Where the fuck are you Abby?" a voice similar to Arun's whispered.

"Excuse me, who is it?" I asked to confirm if it was Arun on the line. All the negative thoughts that had flushed out of my mind when my call to Myra was received, returned to my head. I was not having a good feeling about the call.

"This is Arun here. There is an extreme emergency. Reach Lifeline Hospital right away," he said in a nervous tone.

"Ww... wwhere is Myra? How come you have her phone?" I stammered with a pounding heart scared of his response.

"I.C.U. She met with an accident and is in a very critical condition. Stop wasting even a second and rush. If you can fly, fly and come, Abby. You don't have much time," he replied.

A chilling sensation ran through my body, making my mind numb and my body extremely weak. The worst fear of my life had caught me unawares. My pulse started racing faster than ever. I rushed to my car as fast as my trembling legs could take me, losing my footing every alternate second. I could hear the traffic, people talking, street dogs barking, etc., but amidst all the noise, there was a deadening silence, the kind we sometimes encounter in our dreams. For a moment, it did feel like I was dreaming. Everything around turned blurred, and all that was flashing in front of my eyes was the teary-eyed face of Myra, calling for me.

It was 7 p.m., the peak hour of traffic. Within five minutes, I got stuck in a jam. With Myra's images blinding me every other second, I started bawling inside my car, feeling helpless. I kept honking, but the traffic did not give way. I opened my window and started shouting, "My wife is dying, let me go.... move out of my way... please let me go!" But the people were so self-centered, nobody cared to move their car aside to make way for mine. I got out of my car, crying inconsolably and requested people with folded hands, "Please move your car aside, let me go. I don't have much time...my wife is in the I.C.U." Finally a couple of them stopped their car to let my car pass, but then, the road was jam-packed and I got stuck again within a minute. I did not have the ambulance siren to signal my emergency to everyone so that they could let me go. I noticed that the other side of the road had less traffic as it was opposite to the direction of peak hour traffic. Without thinking about the traffic rules, I drove over the divider to the other side of the road and started moving ahead, only to be caught by a traffic police.

"Sir, my pregnant wife has met with an accident and is in the I.C.U. I need to reach the hospital urgently. Take whatever fine you have to, but let me go. I need to go!" I requested the cop with a sense of urgency.

"If you are trying to weave some fake story, I will put you behind bars," the cop replied rudely.

"I don't have time to prove the authenticity of my words. Just know that I can even kill to be with my wife right now. Let me go!" I told him in a threatening voice as I felt blood gushing into my face.

"Wait right here," he said and went to his senior who was standing nearby.

"Leave your car here and hop onto my bike. I will take you to the hospital faster," he returned to me and said as I looked at him in surprise.

"Don't waste time. Sit!" he continued.

Throughout my way to the hospital, I kept choking back my tears and praying to god, looking up in the sky, "You can't take away my Myra from me bhagwaan ji. Our love story cannot end like this. Please bhagwaan ji, *bacha lijiye meri* Myra *ko*. Please save my Myra. Take everything I have, but don't take Myra away from me. I promise I will visit every temple I come across in my life to thank you if you accept my prayers. I will never ask you for anything in life. Please, please, please..."

"It is all my fault. If something happens to Myra tonight, I will never be able to forgive myself. Why the hell did I change my plan? Oh god, please help me," I cursed myself, crying and banging my forehead with my hand like a mad man.

I checked my phone again and noticed that the missed call from Myra was minutes before Arun's series of missed calls started. This meant Myra wanted to talk to me just before she met with the accident, or maybe, she met with the accident because she was on the phone making a call to me. Had I picked up her call, things probably would have been different. The thought made me nauseated and I felt like I would faint.

"Aaaaaahhhhh!" I shouted in the air in frustration of being too powerless to reverse the time and change things.

"Hi Arun! I am about fifteen minutes away from the hospital. How is Myra?" I called up Arun to get a heads-up on Myra's condition.

"She is still unconscious," he replied.

"I will be right there."

"Abby, there is some bad news. The doctors could not save your baby."

"Noooo… my baby," I wailed as my heart sank. Though I had never met that baby, we still had some sort of a connection because it used to kick inside Myra's tummy whenever I talked to it. My life seemed like a house of cards that had just started tumbling.

"How is Myra?" I asked as my wailing reduced to a whimper.

"The doctors are trying their best to revive her, but they have asked us to be prepared for the worst. The chances of survival are meagre," he said.

"Arun, go to Myra and ask her to fight it out. Tell her that her Abby is coming to give her the strength she is missing to regain her consciousness," I requested Arun.

"I would have, but the doctors are not letting anyone in. You come fast," he replied.

"I am almost there. Ask them to call for the best doctors in the world. I will pay whatever it takes, but beg them to save my Myra. Please Arun, at least tell the doctors this. Do it right away," I said and disconnected the call.

Myra had always been a fighter. Like me, she had too much ego to accept defeat and surrender to any cause or person. The thought gave me a ray of hope that Myra would soon get back to her normal chirpy self with her trademark bursts of laughter.

"Myra, don't you want to read our love story? I have so many surprises planned for you, surprises that will take your breath away. Hold on Jaan, at least until I reach you. Once I reach you and hold your hand in mine, no power will be able to snatch you from me. Just hang in there fighter, I am coming," I closed my eyes and tried talking to Myra, hoping telepathy had some weight in its existence.

Finally, we reached the hospital. I jumped off the bike, thanked the cop and rushed to the reception to ask for the I.C.U. When I reached the I.C.U., a couple of doctors were talking to Arun. As soon as Arun saw me, he hugged me tight.

"What happened doctor?" I asked in a scared voice, gulping the bare amount of saliva that was there in my dried-up mouth.

"We tried our best but... we could not save her. I am sorry," the doctor replied. After a sudden, loud and painful thud, my heart stopped beating for a few seconds.

"What... what do you mean, you could not save her?" I stammered as I felt an invisible knife cut through my heart.

"She is no more," the doctor said in a mournful voice.

A wave of shock brought me down to my knees and shook my soul, shattering me into bits. I felt paralyzed as the world came crashing down on me. I was finding it very difficult to breathe and come to terms with what the doctor had just said.

"You are lying. She cannot leave me like this," I said and entered the I.C.U. only to be greeted by my lifeless Myra lying with her mouth open and eyes closed. Her golden hair was drenched in blood which was also all over her pillow and bed.

"Myra, your Abby has come. Open your eyes," I told Myra, holding her bloody hand that failed to clutch mine back.

"Myra, enough of your drama. These people are thinking that you are actually dead. Get up now. Don't irritate me. I know you are doing this because I hurt you last night. I am sorry Jaan, it will never happen again. It was my fault, I admit it. Any normal person would have reacted the way you did last night. I have some birthday surprises planned for you, which I was telling Shalini about. I kept deleting the chat because you could have read it and got to know about all of them before the right time. You don't believe me? See, the tickets for our Dubai trip later this week. We are going to celebrate your birthday in Dubai," I said and waved the e-ticket on my phone in front of her closed eyes that refused to open.

I had become detached from reality and was behaving weirdly. What else could you expect from a person who had just lost the girl who kept his heart beating? At multiple instances, I felt that all of this was a part of my long nightmare and I was hoping Myra would wake me out of it any moment, with her creaking but my favourite voice, "*Hamesha sotey rehte ho. Jo sota hai wo khota hai.* The one who sleeps, loses. Get up now Mr Lazybones!" But it was not some bad dream; it was happening for real. The person who I was hoping would wake me up was herself sleeping.

"Jaan, please don't do this to me, please. I will always do whatever you ask me to do. I will never argue with you, I promise. You win, I lose. Please wake up Myra. *Utho na… uthti kyun nahi tum?* Why don't you wake up? You don't look good when you are quiet. Come on, speak up, shout at me. It is better to see you yell at me than to see you silent and still like this.

"Since when did you start having such a deep sleep? You normally wake up at the slightest of sound. *Ab kya hua, itna bol rahe hain fir bhi soi hui ho.* Look I got you your novel, the one based on our love story that you have been eagerly waiting to read. See, the cover you designed looks so perfect," I said and showed her the novel, but her eyes still did not open.

"Jaan, I will run away with Shalini if you don't wake up now," I made my last attempt to revive her, but to no avail.

"Abby, she will not wake up. The doctors want to take the body for postmortem. Let them do it," Arun came into the I.C.U. and said, holding my shoulders from behind to console me.

"Arun, I need some time alone with my Myra. Please," I requested.

"Take your time Abby. I will handle the doctors," he said and left.

I lay down sideways beside my Jaan and hugged her, placing one of my legs on her lower body. Whenever I did that, she used to turn to my side and cuddle up to me. But this time, she kept lying flat on her back, motionless and breathless. She smelt of blood as opposed to her Davidoff Cool Water perfume. I buried my face in the nape of her neck and started murmuring with an unbearable pain in my throat and chest.

"Why is your body so cold Jaan? Turn to me and let me warm you up," I said but unlike always, she did not turn to me.

"Jaan, please *uth jao na*. I will not be able to live without you. Don't ditch me like this. I had asked you to hang on. Were you so angry with me that you did not even want to see my face for one last time?

"It really hurts to see you covered in blood. You can't even imagine the agony you are putting me through by lying so still and quiet. I am not used to this. I love you more than anything else in the world. You are my priority and will always be. Come back baby, come back and show me the twinkle in your eyes again.

"You always wanted me to quit entrepreneurship and join a job, right? I have quit it, baby. I sold off Eduwiser, to buy you your dream penthouse in Dubai as a gift for your birthday. And if that is not enough, we are shifting to Dubai within a few months to lead a life you always dreamt of. All your wishes have come true.

"Jaan, you were the sun that lit up my life. Don't leave me in the dark. You have been there with me in everything I have done. Without you, I will not be able to do anything. There is no one in this world who can love me the way you have. Don't leave me alone, please come back, come backkkk, come backkkkkk!" I said as my whimper gave way to uncontrollable bawling. But no matter how hard I tried to entice her, she was not going to come back.

All my life's moments I spent with her started flashing in front of my eyes, breaking me down completely. I felt as if I had become emotionally bankrupt. This was not a temporary loss that could be later made up for. It was a permanent one that was going to leave me with a bottomless pit in the core of my being.

I understand life is a roller coaster with ups and downs, but I felt like I was thrown off the ride when it was at its peak. Life and god could not have been more unfair. The accident came as a thief and stole Myra from me. I was like a football player who had just lost both his legs while playing the match of his life, a mechanic who had just lost both his hands while fixing the car of his life. My life would never be the same.

This was all on me. I killed Myra and I deserved the situation I was in. Had I accompanied her to the sonography clinic, I would have been there by her side to protect her from any mishap. Totally devastated, I abused myself, but it was of no use. It was too late.

As I got up from Myra's bed, I just could not let go of her hand and I kept standing there holding it. I wanted to spend the rest of my life sitting by her lifeless body and talking to her. My life was worthless without her. I had lost my mind and was not in control of my senses. I started looking around for something to help me achieve my latest objective – suicide.

Unfortunately, Arun came back into the I.C.U. right then and sensing my self-harming intentions, took control of me with the help of an attendant. I kept pleading with them to leave me alone with my Myra for some more time, but this time, they did not relent. As they dragged me out of the I.C.U., my tear-laden eyes kept staring at the most beautiful face of the most amazing person in the world.

"Arun, how did the accident happen and who was responsible for it? Tell me and I will see to it that I kill that bastard," I said after regaining composure.

"Abby, we can talk about that later. Right now, Rey needs you," Arun replied.

"I can't go home right now. What am I going to tell him when he asks where his Mumma is? He doesn't even know what death means. Please let him stay at your house for tonight," I requested him.

"He is not at my house. He is in the next room, fighting for his life," he held me and said.

"What? A part of me just died with Myra, now don't kill the remaining with this news… please take back your words," I said as I felt my stomach shrink into a tiny ball. I tried to force my way into Rey's room, but was turned away by the nurses and asked to wait outside.

God was being so cruel. He threw the entire world's sorrows into my lap all at once. I had no idea he had planned to wipe out my whole family in one go. I always used to keep preaching Abby's Fourth Law of Life according to which "*Whatever happens, happens for your best*"; you might not realize it right then, but few days, weeks, months or years down the line, you do, but I saw nothing even remotely good in what was happening with me.

"Wasn't Rey supposed to be at your place?" I asked Arun amidst my breathlessness and free flow of tears.

"He was supposed to be, but he wanted an auto-rickshaw ride, and so Myra said she would take him along with her to the clinic in an auto-rickshaw."

"Fuuuuck!"

"He has lost a lot of blood and is in urgent need of A+ blood. I have called a few of my friends to arrange for it. Getting it should not be a problem, but getting it in time might be. What is your blood group?"

"Our blood groups are the same."

The doctors took my blood sample for reconfirming the blood group. In the meantime, I got a chance to go inside Rey's room. Seeing a cute three-year-old, forever playful boy, who loved me the most in the world, lie in a badly bruised state gave another blow to my already battered soul. Rey was a replica of Myra in looks. When I saw him, it seemed like little Myra was lying there, struggling for her life. I held Rey's hand in mine and started talking.

"Thank you Rey, for waiting for me. I want you to know that your Daddy loves you a lot and he is here for you. Your Daddy will not let you go. Please beta, fight against the odds. Your Mumma has already left us. If you also leave me, there will be no reason for me to continue with my life. I am not praying to god for you, because I don't trust him anymore. If there is anyone who I trust in this world, it is you Rey, and that is the reason I am praying only to you, please don't go!" I said with my eyes flooded with tears.

"I promise you Rey, whoever is responsible for your Mumma's death and for the state you are in, will have to pay for his deed. I don't care if god or the law punishes him in future; I will see to it that we get an eye for an eye, and I fucking don't care if it makes the whole world blind," I said with my clenched teeth, seething with anger.

I gave whatever quantity of blood my little Myra needed to spring back to life.

"What exactly happened, Arun? Tell me everything. Were you there when the accident occurred?" I asked Arun while we were sitting in the hospital lobby, waiting for Rey to regain consciousness.

"I met Myra and Rey at the building reception. Myra told me that Rey wanted a ride in an auto-rickshaw and she was taking him with her in one to the sonography clinic. I was still at the building reception when I heard a loud bang, shortly after which people gathered on the road right outside our building main gate. When I rushed outside, I saw it was Myra and Rey who had been hit by a speeding vehicle and were lying unconscious. The vehicle had sped away by then. I quickly rushed them to the hospital with the help of our building security guard who stands at the main gate," he described.

"Where was my maid? She was supposed to go with Myra. She must have witnessed what you missed. Did she tell you anything?"

"There was no maid with her. Maybe Myra sent her home. But the building security guard did witness what I missed. He told me that Myra and Rey were waiting for an auto-rickshaw by the side of the road. From their left side, a bus was coming, behind which was a speeding Toyota Fortuner that was trying to overtake it. The bus suddenly stopped. To avoid banging into the bus, the car turned right towards Myra and Rey, and hit them. Terrified of being caught, the driver sped away instead of stopping, and in the process, drove over her body. Had he stopped, things would not have been as serious."

"Did the guard note down the registration number of the car?"

"Yes, he did."

"Get me the name of the owner of the car."

"Sure."

Rey started responding well, but was still under close observation. Meanwhile, the cops came to record our statements.

Arun then went to the police station early in the morning to file an FIR. I called up both sets of my parents and asked them to come to Mumbai immediately, citing Myra's ill-health as the reason. As I took Myra's name while talking to them, I choked with emotions yet again.

All of them lived in Patna. So, they reached Mumbai together by the same flight, in the evening. Arun picked them up from the airport and brought them to the hospital where I informed them of the misfortune that had befallen us. As expected, they were distraught with grief and I did whatever I could to console them.

We brought Myra's body home the next day. I had not come back home even for a minute after the accident because I did not have the guts to do so. As I entered our home with Myra's lifeless body, there was dead silence. It seemed as if the house knew and was mourning her loss. When Myra was alive, our household was always a noisy one, with constant laughing and shouting. She had taken away all that with her.

Her night suit that she was wearing the night before the accident was still lying on my bed. I locked myself up in my room and smelled her clothes which still had her fragrance. A piercing pain cut through my body as I buried my face in her clothes and started wailing for the umpteenth time. I packed these clothes in a plastic bag and kept it in my laptop bag, safe and sound, to preserve her smell for as long as possible, thinking that it would make me feel Myra was still with me.

I performed the last rites of Myra as Rey was still recovering in the hospital. It was the height of irony – I lit up and destroyed the very body I had vowed to protect throughout my life. I kept crying profusely as I saw Myra's body turn from flesh to ash.

For the next one week, I stayed in the hospital with Rey, though my relatives and friends offered to fill in for me to give me some rest. I was not ready to budge from Rey's side because I wanted to stand guard over his life. Sleep eluded me throughout the week. As soon as my eyes closed due to fatigue, Myra's face would flash in front of my eyes and I would get up gasping for air, with intolerable heartache and restlessness, knowing that I would never get to see her again.

I brought Rey back home when he got discharged. Completely unaware of the grief that awaited him in the days to come, he was very happy on seeing all his toys. Mom and Dad wanted to stay back longer, but I asked them to leave in a few days, because I wanted to be left alone with Myra's memories.

"It was destiny, beta and you could not have changed it. So, do not blame yourself for what happened. Everything will be fine again. You have to take care of yourself to take care of Rey properly. Get busy with work to give yourself a break from your sorrow. In fact, I think you should come to Patna with us for a few weeks or months, and then take it on from there. We will leave the decision to you. I know our son is strong enough to come out of this bad phase alone, but anytime you think you need us, give us a call and we will take the next flight to Mumbai to be with you," Mom said while leaving Mumbai.

Rey was still not 100% fit and was expected to take a month to be up and running again. After a few days, the inevitable happened and he started asking me about his Mumma, getting only my tears in response. When the frequency of his questions increased, I started giving him vague answers.

"Daddy, I want Mumma," he said one day when I was feeding him.

"Mumma has gone out," I replied.

"She has gone to meet her friends?"

"No, she has gone on a long vacation."

"With her friends?"

"Yes."

"Why didn't she take me with her?"

"Remember she used to tell you that she will run away if you don't listen to her?"

"I will listen to her. Can you call my Mumma back now?"

"Ok, I will tell her."

"Daddy, I want Mumma to feed me."

"I also want the same, Rey. But as I said, Mumma has gone on a long vacation. So, it will be better if we learn to feed ourselves."

"Naughty Daddy! I will not talk to you. I will talk only to Mumma."

"Fine, you talk only to her, but eat."

He missed Myra and so did I. In fact, everyone in this world who knew her as a person, missed her. She always thought Rey did not love her. Had she witnessed how much he asked about her now, she would have been on top of the world.

Ever since I had returned home with Rey, my situation had been worse than one can imagine, unless he has gone through a similar situation. Everything at home had memories of Myra associated with it. All her memories were beautiful, even the ones in which we fought. And these memories often tried to suffocate me to death. However hard I tried, I just could not get Myra out of my mind and the helplessness made me feel as if I would implode.

When Rey resumed going to school, I started getting more free time to myself. During such times, I would open Myra's wardrobe and press her clothes tightly against my chest and face. With my weepy eyes closed, I would imagine myself hugging her while doing so. The fragrance of her clothes gave me some breaths to wade through each day. Relatives had wanted to remove all her belongings from our house, but I had threatened them with dire consequences if they dared to touch any of them.

I still used to find it very difficult to sleep because as soon as I closed my eyes, Myra's images would start playing on the inner side of my eyelids. I could only sleep for a few hours at night and that too after I got a new pillow made, stuffed with Myra's night suit that I had packed in a plastic bag (which sadly could not retain her fragrance for too long). Almost every night, my hands used to subconsciously look for her in bed, but then reality would strike me, followed by a sense of emptiness and a severe pain in the chest.

There was absolute silence in my life, a silence that was more deafening than the loudest explosion in the world. This silence tried to eat me up from within, especially at nights after I put Rey to sleep. When Myra was there, this was the time we spent sitting very close to each other and chatting about everything and everyone. Sitting alone at night, smoking cigarettes after cigarettes, I allowed myself to get sucked into some kind of an emotional black hole, hoping that it would lead me to her.

We had thousands of photos together, saved on my laptop. Whenever I browsed through them, I ended up crying for hours with no one to console me and wipe my tears.

There was no one else in the world who could make me feel complete. Without her, I did not want to do even the most routine things. I always used to eat with Myra. With her gone, I did not feel like eating at all. Even going to the bathroom felt incomplete without Myra banging on the bathroom door and shouting, "Do you have any plans of coming out today?"

Myra used to get restless when I wasn't around. Now, there was no one who looked out for me and sent me "missing you" or "I love you" messages when I would be out. There was no one now who pestered me with her calls to come home early or who hugged me when I got back.

I would often get angry at Myra for being an escapist and disembarking so early from the vehicle of our lives, leaving me to go on alone with no one to guide me. I felt like a mariner lost in a sea without a compass.

I had heard that writing out feelings makes one feel lighter. So I thought of writing an email to Myra one night, listing the questions that were causing a ruckus in my mind. When I opened my email account, I saw an email from Myra that was sent on that unfortunate day. The email however, was blank. I wondered why she sent me a blank email because she did everything for a reason. Maybe, it was to convey that she was thinking of me and wanted me to apologize. Feeling terrible at the thought, I started writing my email to her.

Hi Jaan,

Life has become very tough for us after you left. I will never forgive you for making my life worse than it would have been in hell. Tum bhi *Shalini* jaisi he nikli *(you are no different from Shalini), because you also dumped me, in fact more brutally than she had. I wish you knew how much it destroyed me when you left.*

You tell me, who will wake me up every morning with a kiss? Who will hog my rajma and chicken curry? Who will watch our favourite movies and shows with me? Who will drink and gossip with me? Whose constant but cute blabbering will I listen to? Who will shout at me and fight with me? Who will laugh at my PJs? Who will go for grocery shopping with me? With whom will I go on holidays? Who will sit by my side in the car and give me instructions to drive properly? Who will tell me which girl to check out? Who will resolve my confusions in life? Who will correct me when I do something wrong and make me perfect? Who will force me to finish things on time? Who will motivate me when I am down? Who will come and sit in my lap when I am sitting peacefully? Who will miss me and cry for me? Who will wipe my tears and hug me when I cry? Who will fight the world for me? Who will worry about Rey and me? Who will make our house a home? There are a million things that you were a part of in my life. All of them feel incomplete without you.

It hurts to use 'Myra was' in place of 'Myra is' while referring to you. I wish I could turn back the clock and change things. At times, I think I am jinxed when it comes to love.

You know when I was on my way to the printing press, I had prayed to Ganpati Bappa that the fight we had the night before your accident should be our last fight, and he actually made it our last fight. I asked him for so many things, but he chose this wish of mine to misunderstand and grant so promptly that I did not even get a chance to meet you for the last time. You believed in life after death. Can't you see what Rey and I are going through? I am sure you can. Why don't you do something about it? Give me a solution please, and give me some peace of mind. I know you must be saying that I am only thinking about my situation, not yours. As far as I know you, you must be having the same feelings that I am having; you must be feeling as helpless as I am feeling. You would also be crying every day and every night. Hai na? *I wonder who takes care of you now. What happens if you get scared while sleeping at night? Is someone up there with you to make you feel safe? If you feel hungry, does someone feed you? When you cry, who wipes your tears and makes you laugh?*

I want to be with you, Jaan. Since you are closer to god than I am, can you request him for my early departure to your world?

Your memories keep haunting me day in and day out. Take me away with you, Myra.

Hoping to see you some day. Take care!

LOVE YOU FOREVER,
Abby

I wished Myra could reply to my email from heaven. If god was so powerful, why couldn't he give internet access to people who left the world? Talking about god, I had lost faith in him. The puja room in my house was done away with, despite resistance from my parents. I did not need a god who took my jaan away from me. First, he made us meet. Then, he tested us against the world. When that was done, he tested us against each other. Even then, his experiments were not over, and he eventually called one of us to him because he wanted to see how the other would fight the entire world alone.

It was not just me who kept thinking about Myra all the time. I guess it was Rey too. On most of the nights before he surrendered to his sleep, he would ask for his Mumma.

"Daddy, I want to sleep with Mumma," he would say.

"I have told you so many times, Mumma has gone on a vacation," I would reply.

"Why is she not coming back? Is she still angry Daddy?"

"Yes. Since both of us were naughty boys and did not listen to her, she left."

"I have told you I will be a good boy. Daddy, call her."

"She forgot to take her phone. Now sleep. I don't want any more questions. You have school tomorrow."

"I love Mumma. Daddy, I miss her. I want Mumma!" he would often end his conversation on this note and start crying, making me cry too.

"Mumma loves you too, beta. When you become big like Daddy, Daddy will go to her and bring her back."

✦

Three months had passed since Myra left the world and I was still living my life in a wide awake coma, unwilling to let go of her memories. Its effect was already showing on my health; I had lost fifteen kilograms and looked like a forty-five-year-old when I was just thirty-one. With my failing health and emotional breakdowns every other day, Rey also started getting affected. Mom and Dad noticed this when they visited Mumbai, and forced me to shift to Patna along with Rey.

We were still far from the first hearing of Myra's court case. The driver of the car that had mowed her down was the brother of a big shot politician. Everyone around advised me to drop the case against him as he could harm Rey to threaten me or even get me killed. But how could I let the accused get away with the kind of sin he had committed.

Things improved a little at Patna, but I could not stay there for the remainder of my life because Rey's future could get affected staying in a small town. I decided to shift to Dubai and become a full-time author so that I could work from home and take care of Rey – my little Myra, to make him a good doctor – something that Myra always wanted.

18

September 2016
Dubai

"Mumma... Mumma... I want Mumma...," Rey's cries snapped me out of my flashback.

"What happened beta?" I said hugging him.

"I am scared," he said as he wept.

"I was in my study working on something important. You sleep, Daddy will lie down with you," I said as I lay down beside him and lost myself to my thoughts, while he drifted back to his sleep.

Almost a year had passed since Myra left us. What used to make me furious was that the court case was still going on with the accused out on bail. Shifting to Dubai was a good move, considering that it saved me from my impending death, so that I could look after Rey. I still had emotional breakdowns, but the frequency of such breakdowns had reduced and the will to live for Rey had overpowered my helplessness to succumb to my grief. Myra's first death anniversary was around the corner and I was dead scared of the beautiful but haunting memories of Myra overpowering me again to send me on an irreversible downward spiral.

There was constant pressure from Myra's parents and mine to marry and move on with my life, but I was still not ready for it; I could never be. Not an hour of my life passed without thinking about Myra. I still used the Ray Ban shades she had gifted me on our last anniversary, even though one of its glasses was now broken. After all, it was her last gift to me and I would take it to the grave with me. I did not get it repaired because I could not risk losing it due to anyone's carelessness. It signified my life in a way. It was incomplete. People thought I was crazy when they saw me wearing it before any important meeting, not knowing the real reason behind it. But I didn't care about what they thought.

I was living with so many regrets. Had I accompanied Myra to the clinic despite our fight, she would have been alive. Nothing so worse than not being by her side when she breathed her last. I had made all of her dreams come true, but she did not even get to know about them, leave aside live them. I had written the novel for her, which had now become a bestseller, but she never got to read it and it was only because I had not let her when I easily could have. She always thought Rey did not love her and she left the world unaware of the fact that he did. I wasted so much of our precious time together fighting with her on trivial issues. Lastly, we parted on a bitter note and I did not even get a chance to apologize to her.

I had re-lived almost my entire past in a couple of hours that night and the nostalgia it induced made me feel restless and nauseated. Myra always used to tell me that we should not put years into our lives, we should put life into our years. I would have lived by it too, but only if Myra had still been around with me.

As if I had not reminisced enough about my past, I wanted to read through all the emails Myra had ever sent me. I brought my laptop from the study and sat on the bed next to Rey, who was asleep, to read through her emails. Eventually, I reached her last email, the blank one. While I was staring at the email with love in my tear-filled eyes, Rey took a turn in his sleep and accidentally put his foot on the keyboard of the laptop. I slowly lifted his foot and placed it back on the bed. When I turned to the laptop, a chilling sensation ran through my body giving me goosebumps.

Rey's foot had pressed some random keys on the keyboard that prompted a 'select all' on the email. The email was not blank; it looked blank because Myra had typed it in white font. When the entire text got selected, it became visible. I started reading—

Hi Abby,

I know you will never take the initiative to come and say sorry to me. So here I am, doing it once again. I am sorry for being rude to you last night. I did not mean to be. It is not that I don't trust you; I do, even more than I trust myself. It was just that I thought you still have feelings for Shalini and I got jealous. You know how possessive I am about you.

I am also sorry if I made you think that I would commit suicide. When I threatened you last night of doing something that both of us would regret, I was thinking only about running away from home for a few days and not about committing suicide. Please never tell me to die like you did last night unless you really want me to. I have told you, you should always say good things because you never know which of your statements might come true. I know you said that in anger and didn't mean it. So, it's ok. I know you love me a lot, more than anyone else in this world and will find it very difficult to live without me.

I know you must be feeling sorry too and would apologize to me tonight or tomorrow on your own. I will not mind waiting, especially after what happened last night when you went off to sleep.

I am writing this email in white font because I know some of your secrets which I can neither blurt out because it will ruin your surprise plans, nor keep them within me because that will keep making me feel guilty. Before telling you about them, let me apologize in advance. Last night, I logged into your email to check if there had been any email exchanges between Shalini and you. Though I could not find any, what I did stumble upon instead, took my breath away. I saw an email from a leading Dubai real estate firm in which it had sent you the possession certificate of a penthouse in Dubai and the procedure to transfer it to my name. This also means we are shifting to Dubai very soon. My heart is still pounding with excitement.

As I write this email, I want to kiss you so badly. I want to sing aloud and dance. I am on top of the world right now. You are the best husband, Abby. You made my dream come true.

Before I sign off, I have to make another confession. My curiosity got the better of me and made me read your novel, on the laptop, in June itself. I read the whole of it and it is awesome. Trust me, it will make you a celebrity author. Don't forget to give me the credit for the title and the cover.

Love you the most. I feel like the luckiest and the happiest girl on earth! I know you will get mad at me when you read this email, but I also know you will forgive me sooner or later. Maybe, you will never get to know the content of this email and will always think it was a blank one.

Love you,
Myra

The email caused me to tear up. I cursed myself for saying the words, "Go, die" because they actually came true and I now had to live with that guilt forever, though Myra had let me off for that mistake in her email. On the other hand, I felt a big load come off my head and my heart. It seemed Myra was still with me, watching over me from somewhere, and the thought finally made me make peace with her death. I put my laptop aside and crashed on the bed, hugging my favourite pillow.

"Thank you for your email Myra... thank you for being there... I love you," I said as I surrendered myself to the most peaceful sleep I had had in the last one year.